Life,

from the backseat

by Gabe Branch

Copyright 2008
ISBN # 978-0-578-00621-5

For

Erin
Richard "Dickie" Cox
Denise "Nice"
Denise "Mouse"
Fudd
Little Steve
Rich "Major"
Big Steve (who I didn't really know)
Skater Steve (who I knew less)
Sergio
Brother John
Black John
John the Black
Jon
Paul "Sun-tek"
Quaker
Hugh
Pippi
Roach
Emily
Fran
Pam
Ryan
Cuervo
Bagel
Heather
Matt
Shawn
Scott
Catherine
Ben (who looked better in my leather jacket than I did)
Dave the inventor of "The Other Place"
Valerie my "Smile Chick"
and Doug, sweet Doug…

Frame:

All of this happened, and none of it did. Either answer being as good as the other, it doesn't really matter either way. We are, in the end, the sum total of our experiences with perhaps enough genetic predetermination providing just enough mystery to keep us believing in something outside ourselves. If we are those experiences though, then we owe what we become to those people we choose to spend our time with or without. That's not to say that if you spend your time with thieves then you naturally become one. What is natural any way? But, there is a certain degree of truth in the belief that those thieves might leave something with you. They might leave something behind. A piece, a part. Not a whole, but a fragment of themselves that would then leave you yourself changed. You would not become a thief. But you might still learn to steal. And having learned how to live as a thief, some part of you, however small, would always be a thief; even when all the other parts of you were not.

If I said to you that this was me then I would be a liar. If I said that it wasn't, then I would be a liar again. If I said something in between; then you might believe me. Or you might decide I was making excuses. Which I am.

It eventually comes down to memory. I remember hope and everyone being full of it as if life itself were about to lay at our feet all the riches and unearned accomplishments that we could dream. Now I would ask why, but at the time it seemed only natural that everything would come for us. Why on earth wouldn't it? We felt full of hope, but we were just full of ourselves; and therefore just full of each other. For we are each other. Bits and pieces cobbled together from scraps of other souls in the midst of cobbling themselves together. All of this happened, and none of it did.

This being said, where are we left? We are left looking backwards. Only reflecting. Looking back and defining life retroactively as we ride forward into the future we unwittingly chose for ourselves. Looking forward, looking back, living life, from the back seat.

1

Shawn was a junkie though nobody knew it. Not any particular kind of junkie, mind you, but a

junkie nonetheless. He had just recently become one. Somewhere in the past few weeks he had

crossed the line where his humanity started to disappear and the need began to take hold. He

didn't want anything anymore just a drug, any drug really. Coke was too much and every dime

seemed to disappear along with his cares. The need was all that mattered. And the need was

often fixed at the parties. At a pot party people just gave the stuff away. The bowl just kept

getting packed and passed around. A coke party was like Texas Hold 'Em. It was like some great

game where you tried to get everything out of someone else but give nothing of your own up. It

all had to do with invites and declines. Who was going to be there who might be there and who

was dealing. If Shawn could provide the time and place then the drugs would show and flow just

enough to feed the need without him needing to shell too much out of his own pocket. Though

his pockets were always stuffed by the ever loving, ever hopeful, and blissfully unassuming

momanddad. Of everyone in the world, those two rubes could always be counted on for an easy

score. Total rollovers they were, falling for any story he cared to give about why and how and

wherefore he just couldn't make the rent on his ample allowance and the living expenses of the

city were just killing him. But never mind that he spent nearly every night in a haze fucking

whatever would or could come his way 'cause the day's wasted if you're not' and he always had

the motivation if not the means. Ten grand had gone up his nose that year. It was the best money

he had ever spent without having to earn any of it.

The apartment was the perfect attraction for the local college youth. Just close enough that he

was in classes occasionally but just far enough away that he was off campus and it made for the perfect place to stop by and get high. And there was always reason enough to get high with Shawn. He was the perfect party guy always amiable and never assuming. The dude was just cool and liked to smoke up or get nice whatever, he didn't care. It didn't matter that he seemed a little older, that made him cool. And it didn't matter that he always seemed to have some scheme brewing and "almost, just about" underway because that was just his way. He was a mover and shaker a modern day dream maker and taker and he was always up for anything and everything. And he talked well.

His parties were legend. Often talked about and the stories were told and retold at other parties. Stories of his little shindigs that seemed to grow in infamy without his effort or involvement. There was of course "The Orgy Story" of which there was much speculation and little in the way of hard facts, but it happened under his watch so people were wont to talk. And then of course there was the "dog fucker tape" which always seemed to resurface at random points during the late dwindling hours of the after hours parties. Some people would be quietly standing and talking in a room and suddenly someone would notice that the hip and trendy use of a pornographic video for idle eye candy was actually a film of people having sex with animals. What always fascinated Shawn was not that people were appalled by the scenes but the fact that they stayed and kept watching. They couldn't stop even if some part of them did want to. A bigger part of them needed to see it. A bigger part of them couldn't live the rest of their lives knowing that there were people who had sex with animals without knowing exactly what that would look like. Welcome to decadence, thought Shawn. Damn but he was cool.

-

Outline of a dream:

I take a job in a small mountain town. I have been here before in the dream world but the characters are all unfamiliar to me. The town and the landscape are the same. The main street curves around a rock face and slopes down the side of the mountain into a small valley where the town is nestled. There is a gas station on one side of the road and on the other an empty building with a 'for lease' sign out front. Further into town there are little, quaint houses. I would call them quaint but someone else might call them depressingly small. Typical small town single family dwellings that were popular in the sixties and seventies. They have been sold and resold by different families over the years and despite their various occupants' additions and alterations they all still seem to have that same middle of the road in America generic quality.

In the town there is a glass shop and I work there for a man who seems not entirely happy with my performance but I am getting better and I am very dedicated to my work. I wake up early and work hard at the shop but still he seems a little displeased. I meet and get to know his whole family. He has three children two boys and a girl. The wife is kind and gentle, but quiet. The man is loud and confident and I feel a little intimidated by him. One of the boys is older and in high school; he takes a liking to me. The younger one, maybe in middle school, is a little strange but friendly and I enjoy the fact that he wears a big pair thick goggles all the time. Then there is the little girl. She is about four years old. She is quiet and has a favorite stuffed animal (a rabbit I think) that she carries everywhere she goes and she often seems to be wearing her pajamas.

After what seems like weeks of working in the glass shop the man pulls me aside and says he thinks I should leave. He likes me but I just can't stay and I must go. I don't know what to do so I ask him to coffee and beg him to tell me what I have done to displease him. We go to a small diner across the street from his house.

I really want to keep my job. I say I will work harder and do better, be more dedicated to my work but it doesn't seem to matter to him. A waitress brings coffee to us. She is friendly and blond in a pink skirt and white apron. She is just a little too old for me to be attracted to her but she is still slim and I look at her body anyway. All I can really see is her smile and she disappears after exchanging a few friendly words with the man. She seems more a stereotype of a waitress than an actual person.

I coax him some more about why he wants to let me go. Then his wife comes and sits with us at the restaurant. Then he starts talking. They both do. It seems they had or have another child. Older and living on his own somewhere far away. They don't talk to him anymore. He had a problem. Something that they considered unnatural. An attachment to his stuffed animal toys as a child. Little stuffed toys. He had a lot of them but he never gave them up. He never grew out of his attachment to his toys. They are ashamed of him. He has some sexual hang-up involving the toys and it's too perverse for them to talk about.

I don't really say anything I just accept their story but I still don't understand why I have to go. They tell me that they are seeing signs in their daughter. Signs that she will have the same problem the son does. They are going to have an intervention with her. They are going to take away her toy rabbit. They want me to come too. If I come to the intervention they will let me stay. If I help them take away the toy rabbit they will let me stay with them.

Later the whole family is in their living room and the little girl comes in. The man starts talking about how she shouldn't be carrying around her stuffed toy all the time, she's too big for it. She needs to grow up. He says no one else carries around a toy all the time and he points out everyone in the family and how they don't have a stuffed toy that they spend all their time with. Then he points at her. He points at his daughter and laughs at her. He makes fun of her for needing her rabbit and he laughs. He takes away the rabbit. Then the whole family starts to laugh at her and point. She starts to cry. The dream ends.

-

Ben looked over at Rina and smiled. They had been fucking all morning and now he was hungry. Having just wiped the semen from their last love session off her belly she was balling up the tissues she had used and threw them in the general direction of the trash can in the corner already overflowing with deposits from that morning and dating back weeks. As Ben watched the blurry arc of the tissue's descent he wondered if there might still be tissues in that can from Rina's last lover. It hadn't been that long ago that she was entertaining Shawn up here so it might be possible that there was still trash in there from more than a month ago. The trash can was clearly overflowing and the room looked as if she never cleaned. Not that he did. The cars on the street outside roared thoughtlessly, careless of the pedestrian traffic that was beginning to pick up as the new semester was starting. Rina didn't have classes today so they could spend the whole day together.

"Do you want to robo-trip tonight?" Ben asked.

"Yeah." Rina replied and started to kiss his chest.

"We're gonna need some money." Ben said thoughtfully looking at the ceiling as Rina started moving her kisses down towards his crotch. That's what he liked about her. She was always up for anything

"Let's just steal it from the drugstore." she said, rising up to look at him then dipping back down. The drugstore. Ben always liked that word. It held… possibility. "Yeah, that's great for the robo but I still need some cigarettes and we should get some whiskey." Whiskey was incapable of being stolen as it was locked up behind the counter at the local government controlled liquor store and Ben knew the cigarettes had the same problem, stuck behind the counter.

"Why do we need the whiskey?"

"It makes it better."

"Oh. Well I don't have anything." Rina meant money, she went back to work on Ben.

"I've got a plan. "

"Do you now?" she said sarcastically, knowing that Ben's social security check wasn't going to be arriving for at least another week and he was always hard up for money this time of the month.

"You ever donate plasma?" Ben said and let the fact that she didn't reply go as he laid his head back and thought about Shawn and what might be left of him in Rina's room as she went down on him.

-

Outline of a dream:

I am in my grandmother's house. I am sleeping on the floor and I wake up in the middle of the night. I have a large stuffed rabbit that I bought for myself at a yard sale with my grandmother a few weeks before. My mother was very upset by the purchase of a cloth stuffed animal. She had immediately taken it so she could wash it thoroughly and remove any potential bugs or bacterial contaminants. She hates germs.

 I am looking around in the dark and can't see much. I roll the rabbit over and in the crotch is a vagina. It's a woman's vagina, red and swollen. I begin to have sex with it. The dream ends.

2

Ben looked up at the building on the corner with his one good eye, his face grimacing into a half smile as he searched the front doors and windows for the address. Rina finally gave up and read it out loud to him.

"This is it. Plasma Donation Center. Why the fuck do they call it a donation center when their paying you?"

"Maybe cause blood plasma dealership sounds fucked up. You ate breakfast right?" Ben questioned her as they climbed the five steps of the stoop in front of the clinic. The street outside was dirty and littered with an innumerable amount of partially and completely used cigarette butts.

"I dunno know, maybe. Why?"

"Sometimes they check your blood pressure. If it's low they won't take you. So you need to eat before hand." Ben wished he had thought to say something back at Rina's before they left but he was so hyped about getting a bottle he hadn't remembered until now. He stared at her slim frame silhouetted by the gray blurry expanse behind her. She seemed unbelievably beautiful in the cold gray light.

"I think I had some pizza when you were still asleep. Let's just go." Ben watched her petite frame bounce up the steps past him. What he could see of her he liked. She had slim hips in tight black jeans and a little tank top that only legally concealed her bra-less pert breasts; her long straight black hair made him think of that old poem by the famous guy all the Goths loved. Who was it? Poe. Raven. Sexy.

"Allright. It's your fifteen bucks.", he shrugged hoping that she did get her fifteen bucks, knowing exactly how he would urge her to spend it. "The thing about this place is they mostly get drunks and junkie's or guys like me looking to get a little extra cash cause their check doesn't always cover everything."

"So what?"

"Well you know. You gotta try and look respectable so they think you're clean."

"But I am clean."

"But you look dirty. And you're with me." he leaned back a little and spread his hands wide gesturing towards himself as if this would allow her to see him and their situation more clearly. His dirty jeans and his brown t-shirt with its random holes acquired under the most obscure circumstances; their origins unknown but their presence completely undeniable. He smiled his grimacing smile, hair covering his bad eye. He shifted in his permanently scuffed boots. He came closer towards her. "And if at least your blood pressure's good they won't have any reason to turn you away."

"Fuck you. Let's go. I'm starting to get hungry."

"See."

"Fuck off.", she said opening the doors to the clinic. Ben stared at her butt in the black jeans letting her lead the way. God she had a tight ass.

-

Outline of a dream:

I am walking, talking to a well dressed girl and her family. They like me; I am nervous. Am I dating her? Are we involved? We are all going to see a movie. We are all dressed up for the occasion. I meet her grandmother. The grandmother is unclear and fuzzy. I can't really see her. It's more like I understand an idea of her standing there in front of me as her features morph and blur in and out of different versions of television grandmothers. She's wearing black. We all are. And it's starting to rain.

The girl bends down to do something. Tie her shoe maybe? I hold an umbrella up high and in front of me so I can protect the girl and her grandmother who are walking slightly ahead of me. I start to get wet but I feel good about myself for protecting them from the rain and allowing myself to get wet. I feel like it is a selfless act and it makes me proud. I also feel like this will win me some approval in her family's eyes.

We all keep walking down the sidewalk surrounded by green grass and there is a big brick building that the walk is beginning to curve around. There are two buildings and the walk comes to a place where they meet. The walk expands into a large concrete pad and it is dark behind the two buildings. There is a short alley between the buildings but it is lined by a tall chain link fence on either side that makes the path so narrow we have to squeeze through it single file. I close the umbrella so I can make it through; the rain seems to have stopped.

When I make it to the other side I am alone and the sun is shining. I don't know what happened to everyone else. I am standing on a busy city street and there are cars speeding up the slight incline of the street towards the end of the block. There are a couple of moderately sized trees coming out of the sidewalk, and there is garbage in large piles spaced at regular, lumpy plastic covered intervals.

There is a large package delivery truck double parked at the end of the block and I see a group of young teenagers standing behind it. The delivery man is gone and the kids are pushing stacks of packages out onto the street and into the cars as they come speeding up towards the end of the block. When the cars stop and the drivers get out, the kids run out from behind their hiding place and attack them. They don't beat them severely; just enough to rough them up and hurt them a little. I start to yell at the kids because I recognize a couple of them, but they don't really listen to me and I soon get distracted by a large pile of garbage.

 In the garbage is a box of shoes. The shoes are all old bowling shoes in varying colors. They are worn out and cracked from age and lack of care. There are leaves and old rags and bits of unidentifiable fluff in the box. I get excited and start looking for a pair in my size. The first pair I pick are too big but I like the faded orange coloring. I throw them aside. I find a faded number on the heel of one shoe that matches my shoe size; I find the shoe's mate. Now I have a pair that will fit me. I am suddenly disgusted by myself and my desire to take these shoes from the garbage. I put the pair down and stand up. The dream ends.

-

"The thing about robo-tripping is, everything is just weird." Ben was staring at the other people in the waiting room of the plasma donation center trying to keep his voice just loud enough for Rina to hear it. "I don't know if it's the liquor or the weed that makes it that way but you put them together and everything just goes crazy." he slouched further into the yellowed plastic chairs provided by the Plasma Donation Center and stretched his legs out in front of him. The fluorescent lights of the brown and yellow waiting room made it hard for him to focus his eye on the other donors but they seemed to be the usual fare of older drunks and homeless looking to pick up a little spare money for a couple of bottles and some cigarettes in between meals. He knew most of them floated around from shelter to shelter picking up a bed or a meal where they could; the cash was all fun money, such as it was. He himself had often needed to do that for a few weeks before his check kicked in.

"What do you mean?" Rina asked back not really looking around the room much, trying to avoid eye contact with the mostly male and seemingly unwashed plasma donation clientele. They didn't really look at her and she tried to avoid them, instead concentrating on Ben and his well muscled albeit nearly blind frame next to her. She sat sideways in her plastic chair which angled her hips to face Ben and allowed her to lean in close to his side where she rested her head on his hard shoulders.

"I mean it just gets weird, it's not like dosing but it is, you know?" Rina shook her head but Ben failed to notice and continued talking as Rina rested her hand on his flat stomach. "It's like, you don't think right. You know; like you turn off a part of your brain but you're still there, like you're asleep but not. Everything seems fuzzy and whenever you look at anything it's like that thing shouldn't be there, but it is anyway."

"That doesn't make sense, baby." Rina said rubbing his stomach in little slow circles and almost nuzzling into his neck as she spoke.

"Yeah, like nothing makes sense. Even if you think you understand it. Hey are you going to sleep?" Ben asked.

"Nope and I mean what you are saying doesn't make any sense. And I'm just getting comfy. I like it when you wax philosophical even if it's all crackpot theory." Rina replied sweetly.

"Anyway," Ben continued not wanting to be interrupted in the middle of his soliloquy on drug usage and its peculiarities, "it's like you don't really see it, you see an idea of it that doesn't add up to anything. And you can't understand anything." he held his hand in the air for emphasis cradling and sometimes pointing to imaginary objects.

"Still doesn't make any sense. Damn baby, you're so hot." Rina said this as quietly in Ben's ear as she could while she let her hand stray closer to his crotch.

"Thanks." Ben replied feeling a growing tightening in his pants as he slid up just a little in his chair to gently push Rina off of him and avoid getting a full blown erection. "Thanks baby, but wait just a bit okay?"

"You know I will, I just like to see you squirm." she said trailing her hand back up to his chest.

"Yeah right. Anyway tonight's going to be fun."

-

Outline of a dream:

I am wearing a suit and I am downtown somewhere. There are buildings all around me. Skyscrapers, such as they are here in town. I am walking down the street. I have to be somewhere soon. I am not late though, I will be right on time. I am a lawyer. I am in a gray suit. I feel well dressed and confident. Do I have a meeting? Am I meeting a client? I don't know. It is morning time; there is a gray and overcast look to everything around me. The sky is gray, the concrete buildings are all gray, and I am in my gray suit. There is a light gray fog in the air and few people on the street. Despite the colors I am happy. Really truly happy and self-confident. The dream ends.

3

"Did you hear about the OJ guy?" Shawn's accent framed the words almost regally in Ben's ears. Ben had sent Rina off to the store to buy the robo for their mutual trip tonight. He, meanwhile, had gone over to Shawn's house. Ben still hadn't eaten and he knew he should before he dived into the brand new fifth of green label he was going to get at the store, just as soon as he asked Shawn to drive him there. Maybe Rina would get something to eat when she picked up the cough syrup. God, he hadn't had anything to eat since that damn cookie they gave him at the donation center. He was starting to feel woozy.

"Oh yeah the guy that thinks he's a big glass of orange juice and he runs around all afraid that somebody is going to tip him over." Ben smiled at Shawn, even though it was half obscured by the hair in front of his face. Ben always wore his hair in front of his bad eye to keep people from staring. Not that Shawn would stare. It was just habit.

"Oh yes, he lives in some mental institution somewhere." Shawn said assured of the truth of his own words. He reached toward Ben and handed him a small brass pipe packed with weed, being careful to place it firmly in his half blind friend's hands.

"I met a guy once who used to stamp his foot on the ground all the time." Ben accepted the bowl and took a long, rich hit that he held in for a few seconds before exhaling and continuing his story through curling smoke. "It was like a twitch. I asked him what was wrong with him. I just figured it was some weird tick you know but he said that there were these little men who lived underneath the ground that would pull on this invisible string that ran from his right ear all through his body down to his right heel and into the ground. And he had to stamp his foot if they started to pull too hard and hurt him."

"Why did they pull on the string?" Shawn asked as he reached back for the pipe with as much decorum as he could muster in the dank and dimly lit surroundings of his apartment's basement.

"To get him to do what they wanted." Ben replied as he gave up the pipe.

"Such as?" Shawn queried, he was always using phrases like that. 'Such as' instead of 'like what'. It had a tendency to make people think he was smarter than he was.

"He never said. He just stamped his foot to confuse them so they would run away and leave him alone. But they always came back." Ben replied and waited patiently for Shawn to finish his hit. As Shawn raised up from being bent over the bowl with his lighter he half coughed his reply of, "Dude, that's fucked up." He blew the smoke slowly out in to the air above him. Ben reached out his hand for the bowl hoping to get another hit before Shawn put it away. It was Shawn's house and Shawn's bag so standard pot rules applied. Shawn decided when the bowl got packed and when to put it away.

"I know, right?" Ben said grasping the bowl Shawn had just placed in his hand and pausing while he finished his thought. "It's like your brain's a computer that's running some program. And the first line of the program is 'I', and the second line is 'I am'," Ben started to gesticulate with his hands, still holding the bowl and was getting more and more excited. "And the next is 'I am a', and the next is 'I am a human', you know and everything else just follows. But the OJ guy rewrote his program. Like, he tripped too hard and went too far and rewrote "I am a human" with 'I am a glass of OJ', you know?"

"So what did the string guy's program say?" Shawn questioned, more out of a need to fill the silence between them as Ben took his hit than from any solid desire to hear Ben go on with his marijuana philosophy.

"I don't know, 'I am a guy with a string from my head to my heel and all these invisible guys are fucking with me'?" Ben replied in a questioning joke, dismissing any further comment on the subject.

"Fucked up." Shawn said taking back the bowl and accentuating the curse word and making it sound even more offensive to Ben's ear because of the accent.

"No shit." Ben replied.

"So how are you and Rina doing?" Shawn finally brought up the subject they had both been avoiding.

"Good I guess. You really okay with everything?" Ben asked a little awkwardly, though even if Shawn hadn't been okay with anything, he wouldn't have stopped seeing Rina.

"Fuck yes. Like I care." Shawn threw his hands into the air for emphasis. "I was just a rebound guy anyway. She wanted to dump her boyfriend and I was just around you know?" Shawn ended his last remark with a wink and a nod in a decidedly English manner. He seemed almost a caricature of all things English to Ben.

"Yeah yeah." Ben noticed that the bowl had disappeared and was feeling a little un-secure with the present conversation.

"She really likes you though." Shawn said and it almost seemed to Ben that Shawn was attempting to convince himself of something.

"Whatever man. I am just along for the ride. That girl's too hot for me even I can see that." Ben replied noncommittally.

"Yeah, her ass is fucking amazing man. And those sweet dimples just above her butt on the small of her back.", Ben wasn't exactly sure how to feel about his friends intimate knowledge of his girlfriends anatomy but he had too admit that Shawn had taken notice of one of Rina's most attractive features. No doubt Shawn had noticed that particular feature on Rina's slim frame while she was bent over in front of him and… Ben pushed the image of Shawn and Rina fucking out of his head and focused on the moment in front of him though it was hard to do through the very good weed Shawn and he had just smoked.

"Like I said man, she is too hot for me and I am just waiting around till she realizes it."

"Is she coming over tonight?"

 "Yeah. As soon as she picks up the robo."

"Good for you man."

-

Outline of a dream:

 I am holding a frog out of the water as if I have just grabbed it and pulled it out. The air around me is clammy like it has just rained and smells like the forest behind my grandfather's house. There seems to be a mist in the air and I am sitting beside a little stream of slow moving water or a small pond. The frog is not moving as I hold it in the air and I notice there is a turtle biting down on the frog's right hind foot. I am holding the frog by one of its front legs and I pull it up closer to my face to see it and the turtle better. The dream ends.

-

 Lil Jim and Berto were walking back from the hardware store, heading down Broad Street and carrying brass treasure in their pockets. The blue bins of the hardware store that carried the brass pipe fittings and connectors had taken some time to navigate. This morning's wake and bake hadn't helped the cause but at least they had accomplished all that they had set out to do today. The new pipes were ready to be filled and passed.

 "Man, I'm getting hungry." Lil Jim broke the silence that had set on them in the hardware store's checkout lane.

"Me too. And I'm a little tired." Berto responded from his mid afternoon daze. The sun always seemed a little too bright all day long when he woke up and baked first thing. He preferred getting high on cloudy days. The light didn't get all fucked up on cloudy days.

"The bowls are cool." Lil Jim piped in with another attempt at conversation. He did like Berto, and almost looked up to him. He believed Berto to be a slightly cooler person and therefore slightly higher on the social ladder. Hanging out with Berto was good times. At least girls talked to him. At least he got laid. Lil Jim was hoping to get Berto's help in this department. Maybe some advice. Maybe just some leftovers.

"Yours is a little wonky dude." Berto said flatly. He stared at the concrete walk and his feet as they moved over it, thinking back to the blue bins and remembering how Lil Jim had gone to great pains to put together a number of pipe pieces and connecting joints to construct a convoluted path for the smoke to follow as the user inhaled. Berto had just made a straight pipe with a large shotgun on the front just underneath the bowl. The bowl would deliver a harsh hit but Berto kind of liked it that way. He didn't want his bowl to look goofy; he just wanted it to work.

"I think it's neat." Lil Jim repeated the answer he had given in the hardware store. Berto had already informed Lil Jim that he didn't approve of the strange and expensive contraption Lil Jim had put together at the blue bins. Lil Jim pretended not to care.

"It's like, way too complicated." Berto replied just a little more coherently.

Lil Jim spoke up in a self reassuring tone. "I'll smoke out of it."

"You'll be smoking alone." Berto said laughing and looking above Lil Jim's short frame at the cars speeding along the street in front of him, waiting to cross.

"How many more blocks is it?'" Lil Jim asked changing the subject from Berto's assessment of his new bowl.

"I don't know. Four or five." Berto said. But Lil Jim knew he always estimated four or five blocks for just about any distance over one block. Berto's sense of measurement and time were both being attacked by his constant inebriation.

"You want to get some food?" Lil Jim said still pushing his conversational boulder in front of him and trying not to doubt the excessive purchase he had made at the store. But his paranoia began to overwhelm his belief in the wonky bowl. What if people made fun of him? Berto already was and he was more sympathetic to Lil Jim's problems than most everybody. What if they all hated it?

"Yeah, let's go to the Village and see who's there. How much money have you got?" Berto said still standing on the street corner waiting for the traffic to stop.

"Some." said Lil Jim and he started to cross knowing that if he waited for Berto they could be there all day. Berto wasn't very good at crossing streets when he was high. He couldn't judge the distance and speed of the cars right, and therefore could never correctly time his crossing.

"Maybe we should get a bag." Berto followed across the street.

"Sure. Who's got?" Lil Jim said as Berto sped up a little to walk just in front of him though still off to his side. Lil Jim had to almost stretch forward as he walked to catch Berto's occasional glances.

"I don't know. Let's just talk to Fat Jenny." Berto glanced over his shoulder. Berto always walked this way with Lil Jim, looking over his shoulder occasionally as he talked but rarely making sustained eye contact.

"She probably has, she usually does."

After a few more blocks and changing streets they came into view of the Village. They entered through the front door by the bar and did the long walk down the one greasy aisle past waxy brown booths in order to see who was at the Village this afternoon. No one they knew or wanted to know was ever at the bar. The only people sitting there were the old bums and the alcoholics that lined up in the morning in front of the place before it opened. It was the only place to get a beer or a drink served up at eight in the morning. It was a sad mournful place up at the front of the café filled with dejected drunks and inattentive wait staff counting their tips and totaling checks. Berto much preferred the back.

Berto put on as cool a look as he could considering his baby face and utter lack of muscle tone. Even Lil Jim, who followed in behind him, had a more defined body than Berto. They darted their eyes back and forth from booth to booth as they walked looking for friendly faces. They found familiar ones but not so familiar as to be friendly. These faces were just the regulars; the backdrop denizens of their insular city dwelling world. These people were always here, in one form or another. They were the same old same olds shuffling up and down the street, standing in front or behind them in the convenience store, wandering in and out of random parties.

Berto and Lil Jim didn't know any one of them but they knew all of them. They had seen their faces a hundred times but didn't know their names. They recognized their changing hairstyles and rotating wardrobes but only knew them by locale. They were passersby on the streets as they moved through the circles of their days, coming together and splitting apart.

They didn't see anyone they knew so they walked down to the second level. A small area in the back that recessed into the floor a few steps down with a wait station and the men's bathroom. They took the middle booth and Berto faced the bathroom and the old unused barber's chair that sat in a small corner too small and close to the bathroom for a table. Something had needed to fill the space and Berto guessed the barber's chair was as good as anything. No one ever sat in it sober. They waited for a waitperson. Waiting to get noticed in the downstairs they looked over the menus as they kept a lookout for anyone they knew. Someone would come by eventually, someone always did.

-

Outline of a dream:

I go upstairs to D's apartment. Maybe I am already up there. I remember walking through the door. But the apartment is not hers. My family is all there. I don't know if we live there or not but everyone is there. Mom and Dad and my brother. They are laughing and talking with each other. They gesture to me. I smile and start to say something but it only comes out as gibberish and they can't understand it. I try to speak again and again it comes out garbled and seems muffled. I begin to get scared and feel like my mouth is full of something. Like cotton but it doesn't make it dry, like glue but it doesn't make it sticky. Everything I say comes out garbled and unintelligible as a result. I start to scream. I scream at them in muffled groans and gibberish. I am pleading with them to understand but they can't. They don't know what I am saying and just keep on laughing and talking with each other. They smile at me as if there is nothing wrong and I scream at them again and again. My ears start to pound and blood is rushing to my head. I am losing my mind. I am terrified. I can't explain it. No one understands me. No one can even help me. I wake up groaning in my sleep and sweating.

4

The two NOVA punks stood outside the back door to Shawn's apartment. They had walked up a short little landing of stairs and were now staring at a rather nondescript door with a very small sign reading 'Department of Parks and Recreation'. Denny looked over at Jack confused.

"Are you sure this is it?" Denny asked.

"Yeah, Shawn said this was it. He said we could come by and smoke up sometime if we wanted.", Jack replied in his quick and snappy voice that carried just enough edge to sound tough despite seeming to be a little high in pitch for a young man of his bulk.

Denny, on the other hand was a great deal taller and thinner than Jack with a much deeper and slower voice. They were often seen together and made quite the odd looking almost Abbot and Costello-like pair, even with their mismatched mohawk haircuts which proclaimed their allegiance to all things punk.

"Yeah but the sign says…" Denny started in forming the words slowly and carefully thinking things over as Jack cut him off in mid sentence.

"You fuckin dumbass. It's a joke." Jack's voice chirped into higher octave as he let out his woodpecker laugh. It was a high giggle punctuated by machine gun serrations of sinister delight. His skinny pink mohawk bounced with his voice.

"What's a joke?" Denny asked. The shorter and decidedly more conservative mohawk on Denny's head didn't bounce when he did anything. It didn't move at all.

"Your mother's a joke." Jack's piercing giggle dropped back down an octave so his voice could retain its aggressive edge. He jerked his thumb towards the door in front of them. "The fuckin sign. Somebody stole it. From school." he stressed his last statement with a sarcastic tone which

Denny, already too high to carry on much of a conversation, missed entirely.

"Oh." Denny knocked on the door.

"Fuckit man." Jack gave up trying to communicate with Denny hoping that whoever answered the door would be a more interesting conversational partner. He slouched against the wall.

-

Outline of a dream:

I am walking. There are some trees but the way is mostly clear and I am walking on grass going uphill. There are other people around me. There are hundreds of them. All of them are walking up the slight incline of this hill with me. There is a light just over the horizon and behind the trees. I can't tell if it is dawn breaking or if it is just a really intense light. It seems white and then it seems yellow like dawn, or sunset. I have been here before. I can't remember when. The people seem well dressed. Am I well dressed? We keep heading towards the light. The dream ends.

-

Lil Jim had spent most of his life wishing. Wishing to be big. His father had been short. Of course growing up lil Jim hadn't ever noticed. But when he got to high school, and puberty and hormones had blessed all his friends with height and body hair, he had felt cheated. He was short. And not just short but small. Light. Weak. Easy to push around. He would have gone out for sports, but he was too small. He would have loved to be one of the in crowd, but he was a freak. In the end he would have loved to just have a girlfriend but he was too small and one of life's first harsh lessons for him was that even small women want big men.

He would dream sometimes that some heretofore unknown or inactive enzyme in his glands would suddenly kick in and he would grow a foot and a half overnight. He would suddenly be big. Or at least normal sized. Then the girls would look at him. Then they would pay attention to him. Then they wouldn't ignore him and snicker when his back was turned.

He knew what they thought and laughed about behind his back. Their great unspoken assumption surrounded and infuriated him. Behind everyone's eyes, behind everyone's smile he saw the question. 'How big is his dick?' ' Is it tiny like him?' 'Is it … proportional?' He knew they thought it. They weren't really wrong. His dick was small. A little dick for a little man. And it pissed him off even more.

He watched the smiles, the stares. He watched as couples disappeared together from all the parties and gatherings while all he could do was drink more, smoke and listen to the tales of hookups and sweaty embraces the next day. All he wanted was to fuck and all he got was drunker and a lonely walk home free from the hang-ups of the opposite sex's affections. God he wanted to fuck so badly. To get laid. When would it ever happen? How could it? No woman wanted that tiny dick.

-

Outline of a dream:

I am in my apartment. But it doesn't look like my apartment. It looks like a hotel room or one of those big housing development style apartments where they carpet the floor and everyone lives in exactly the same floor plan. If not the one, then the reverse of that. All white walls and brown carpet and mini-blinds. It feels like a hotel.

There is someone in here. I don't know him but he came with someone I do know. Whoever I did know is gone and they left him behind. He's big and aggressive. He won't leave me alone. Is he trying to pick a fight? Does he want to beat me up? He has such a big face and he stands at least ten inches taller than me. I scream at him to get out but he just smiles and smiles. I hate his smile and big square jaw. He is actually attractive. More attractive than me and in better shape. I envy him and he is being cruel to me. I don't know how but I sense a lot of malice from him. I keep screaming at him to get out but he keeps refusing.

 I hit him right in the nose. I hit upwards and push back trying to break his nose and shove it into his brain like I have seen in the movies. He falls down flat on the floor. I think I have killed him. I am so happy. I sit down to read until my significant other gets home to help me move the body. I can't remember who my significant other is but I know I wanted the big man out of the apartment because I was afraid of what he would do when they got home.

 When I hear the door open, I look up from what I was reading to call out to my significant other but I immediately notice that the body is gone. The big man is still alive, and he is somewhere in my house. I run to the door to tell my companion not to come in, that it is too dangerous, but I find them both in the same front room. The big man is laughing.

I attack him and he grabs me and holds me. He is incredibly strong I hit him in the nose again and again trying to break it and kill him but he just keeps laughing. He smiles with his big face and laughs at me as he holds me by one arm and lets me hit him with the other. He can stop me anytime. I can't hurt him at all. He keeps smiling and I keep trying to kill him. The dream ends.

-

 Berto wanted things. Big things. And lots of them. He had a little cash and Fat Jenny was gonna pay off. He and lil Jim had waited for a good hour before anyone they knew had shown up at the Village but eventually came in Fat jenny. Big beautiful Fat Jenny and she was packing. Or at least she had some at home. So they had finished their fries, greasy and sloppy with loads of ketchup and salt. Slurped down the rest of their coffees and followed Jenny home.

"These are what I got." Jenny said pulling a large dried bud of marijuana out of a pill bottle she pulled out from under her ample bed. "And baby its sooo kind." Jenny drawled her speech out a little more than necessary in a self reflective sarcasm making fun of her own stoner talk.

"Sweet.", Berto replied, he loved when Fat Jenny did her stoner talk. He reached out for the bud and brought it up to his nose inhaling deeply. The rich aroma of a promising high enticed him greatly. "I'll take it."

"Goody gum drops!" Fat Jenny exclaimed back to him in a sing-song childish voice and took the twenty he held out to her. Berto didn't bother to have Jenny weigh it out. He knew she always gave him a little more than what he paid for and she always smoked him up when his funds were running dry. Jenny smiled as Berto pulled out his brass construction from the hardware store.

"Let's break in this new bowl I just made." Berto said smiling devilishly knowing where getting Fat Jenny and Lil Jim high would get him.

Fat Jenny smiled back as she pulled some weed out of her private stash to pack the first round with. She had been hoping Berto would stick around today. They had been fucking off and on for about a month now and she liked him. She liked him a lot more than any of the other guys she was occasionally seeing. Berto was sweet even if he was clueless sometimes. They'd all get high and then she and Berto would sneak off together for some fun. Goody gum drops she thought.

-

 It was about six o'clock now and Berto was rolling off of Fat Jenny for the second time. He was sweating heavily and she was covered in more than one of his bodily fluids.

"Damn." he said. "That was awesome."

"Thank you." Fat Jenny replied reaching towards the bedside table overflowing with empty cigarette packs, very full ashtrays and wads of toilet paper containing the comings and goings of Berto from the last month.

Lil Jim was still passed out in the living room and probably would be for another hour or two.

"Whatcha want to eat?" Berto asked.

"I don't know, I've got some pasta and sauce. And some leftover meatloaf that my mom sent home with me." Fat Jenny offered up the meatloaf reluctantly but she knew that Berto was always starving after he fucked her. Oh well, he deserved it. He was a skinny rascal but he could really work it in the bedroom. And he would go down on her anytime she asked. She figured she could part with the meatloaf.

"Meatloaf." he said the word and she could almost hear him salivate. "Homemade meatloaf." Berto pulled on his pants and shirt. He gave her a little peck on the cheek as she was getting dressed and headed for the kitchen. She sighed when he left the room.

-

Outline of a dream:

I am a soldier. Maybe I am not a soldier but I am watching soldiers? I can't tell, but there is a lot of green. I don't feel stressed though. I feel calm. Protected, secure and completely without need or desire. I am not nervous at all. We are moving. A lot of us. It's confusing and there are droning roaring noises all around. Everything is blurry, but I am happy.

-

Lil Jim twitched in his sleep and mumbled something completely incoherent. Berto was afraid that he had let Jim smoke too much but there was nothing he could do about it now. Lil Jim always smoked too much. He drank too much, smoked too much, tripped too much, talked too much. In short, lil Jim was too much. If Jim had been of a normal stature, and not just under five feet, Berto wouldn't worry so much about him, but Jim wasn't of a normal stature and Jim hated it when anyone pointed this out. Berto had tried to slow down his drinking at parties. Gently implying that someone might not want to drink to such excess with as slight a frame as his but this just made Jim drink even more, if only to prove that he could handle it. Which he clearly could not. Berto decided to stay out of things from then on. He figured he knew why Lil Jim drank so much anyway.

Berto figured that Jim was just so pissed about being small and so in need of a lay that he felt like he had to make up for it by partying twice as hard as everyone else in the room never mind the fact that lil Jim rarely made it to the end of a party. 'It's not good to go into a party with something to prove" Berto thought, but there was little he could do about Jim and his excesses. Jim wasn't happy and the only thing that was going to make him happy was getting laid but Berto figured that was about as unlikely as Jim suddenly growing a foot taller. So that meant lil Jim was stuck. Forced to trudge along as a little man. His shortcomings (Berto giggled to himself at the pun) plainly visible to the entire world.

Truth was lil Jim was stuck in a vicious cycle. Jim was pissed about being small. He wanted to get laid so bad that it made him seem desperate. This meant that every time Jim even spoke with a girl she could tell immediately that he only wanted to bed her. Which Berto knew was exactly what every guy wants to do it's just a matter of how well each one of them is able to hide it. But Jim couldn't hide it. He might as well carry a sign. So this meant that at every party lil Jim went to, he followed the same pattern. He walked around, tried to talk with girls. He offended them by being too aggressive. Got pissed because they started to ignore him. Then got obnoxious. Then they ignored him even more. Then he started to drink more. Then he got more obnoxious. Then he became incoherent. Then he drank so much he couldn't stand up. Then he passed out. It happened all the time.

Lil Jim was a nice enough guy when he was sober. He was kind of an idiot when he was drunk.

And he was downright belligerent when he felt like no one was paying any attention to him. And people ignored him often. Berto was ignoring him now, letting him stay asleep on the living room couch as he and Fat jenny watched TV in her bedroom eating the last of her mother's meatloaf. Berto hadn't bothered to wake Jim as he heated up the meatloaf in the microwave in Jenny' kitchen. He didn't really want to share the meatloaf with lil Jim anyway. Berto wasn't even sure if Jim knew that he and Jenny were sleeping together on occasion. Poor lil Jim. Oh well, his loss.

-

Outline of a dream:

I am wandering in someone's house. It's large. Has two floors. The floors are made of old wood. It's all dry and cracked. The floors are gray. An old aged gray. The kind of gray wood gets when its been outside in the rain for years on end. The walls of the house are painted white. Thick layers of paint. Again old.

I see people. Mostly just glimpses of them. They talk around me. At each other. I can't really understand them. I want to appease them. Make them happy. I think I, we, are all searching for something. Something in the house. I keep wandering. Looking for something though I don't know what.

I come to the end of a hallway. It seems there are stairs to the right and an open room to the left. I look in. There is a big window and the sun is shining in. It seems like morning time. The sun is so bright I almost can't see anything in the room. Then I see it. A huge pig in this room. Tied up to something in the corner. I can't see what. But the pig is wearing a bow. A yellow bow around its neck. The dream ends.

5

Shawn wasn't English. Everybody kind of knew that because he claimed to have come from North Carolina and when he drank too much he would occasionally slip into a deep and undeniably southern accent. He would also slip into this accent when he got very angry but no one ever saw Shawn angry. He didn't allow it.

No one was quite sure where he had gotten the almost English accent though and no one liked to question him too much because he always evaded their probes and inevitably turned the tables on them by making bizarre references to great literature classics that no one in his inner party circle had read. In short Shawn just got weird when you asked him about himself and his past. All anyone really knew about him they gleaned from off-hand remarks he made when he was drunk. Shawn seemed to have all the money he needed. He lived in a dive but he never went hungry, always had weed or beer and never worked. No one knew how much money he did have; they just knew he had enough.

That accent was still a mystery though. It wasn't quite English per se but it bore a strong resemblance. Only Ben really knew where it had come from and he wasn't going to tell anybody. He had no reason to expose Shawn for what he was, just another rich fag from NC. Ben knew Shawn was putting on airs and he didn't care. Ben loved him.

Knock. One knock? Ben looked over at the door. He was in Shawn's kitchen attending to a can of baked beans he had managed to rifle out Shawn's exasperated cupboard.

Knock. Shit there it was again. Where the fuck was Shawn? He said he was going to check the mail. A task Shawn often attended to infrequently if at all as it required him to move his bed from in front of the front door of his apartment and exit out towards the front of the building which faced out on Floyd Ave. Shawn didn't like using his front door but his bed placement had had more to do with maximizing space in his tiny living room than not wanting to use the front entrance. Anyone who knew Shawn came to the back door through the alleyway. Only Mormons and momanddad came to the front.

Jack and Denny straightened a little as the back door to Shawn's apartment opened up to reveal a dirty kitchen containing an aging stove, a couch sitting with its back to the door and a television sitting on an antique dining table that had anyone ventured to get it appraised would have been revealed to be and early Shaker piece with an estimated value of around two thousand dollars. Had Shawn, or Ben, or any of their friends ever realized the worth of the table they would have immediately sold it for the cash. No one did realize of course, which is why the table remained where it stood; holding up a television and various dirty dishes.

Jack peered into the kitchen past Ben and asked,"Shawn here?"

"Yeah, he's out checking the mail." Ben replied still standing in the doorway. He held a half opened can of baked beans in his right hand, the can opener still perched on the top waiting to finish opening Ben's foraged meal.

"Can we come in?" Jack asked with a little bite in his voice sensing that he could push Ben around a little if he wanted to. Ben's bad eye and now stoned demeanor, added to the fact that Jack was easily much broader in the chest than Ben, made Jack feel superior and so he took the upper hand.

Ben just nodded and backed into the kitchen opening the door further allowing both Denny and Jack to enter. Ben didn't ask them who they were. He didn't care. Shawn always had more people over than Ben could keep track of, and every year the faces changed. Ben had known Shawn for three years now and the two of them were just about the only constants in each other's lives. Everyone else just finished school or moved away, on to better things. The faces changed but the parties didn't. It was something to do.

-

Shawn did like Floyd Ave. It was mostly quiet and really close to the university so there was always some hot chick walking down the street. His small apartment building also had the exclusive pleasure of being located in between a daycare for children and a group home for mentally challenged adults. There was a fraternity house on the corner that held beer drenched gatherings every other Friday. Shawn's place, being a short walking distance from it through the parking courtyard in the alley behind the block, always seemed to attract a few of the more adventurous party goers in the aftermath of the frat house keggers.

Shawn rifled through the mail left in a disordered heap next to the antique over-painted radiator in the commonly shared hallway of his apartment house. There were four apartments in the building; two upstairs and two down. Shawn's upstairs neighbors had come to parties at his house on at least three occasions but he could not for the life of him remember what any one of the looked like. Shawn knew his downstairs neighbor intimately owing to an un-patched hole on his neighbor's bathroom floor and Shawn's open access to the basement of the entire building. Shawn had first discovered this unfortunate bit of home decay while his neighbor, with whom he had never actually spoken, was stepping out of his shower. Shawn did on occasion stray to boys but fat old men with gray hair on their ball sacks was another thing entirely. Shawn shuddered remembering the incident. There is nothing quite like seeing a grown naked man drag a towel back and forth across the underside of his crotch from underneath.

Shawn walked back into his apartment to find Ben eating cold beans from a can and clearly not intending to save him any. Ben looked up at Shawn. Shawn looked at the two Nova Punks standing awkwardly while Ben hunched over his can on the floor of Shawn's living room slash bedroom.

"He let us in.", Jack jerked a thumb towards Ben and Shawn just nodded.

"Can we smoke this here?" Jack produced a bag of weed from his pocket and Shawn smiled. Sure man. Sure. Shawn closed the front door of his apartment and pushed his bed back in front of the door. He led the punks into the little hallway between the kitchen and the living room, past the bathroom, and to the rickety door that gave him and thus everyone he knew access to the basement of his little apartment house.

The basement ran the length of the building but Shawn only utilized the space directly underneath his own apartment. Partly because there wasn't any electric lighting in the rest of the basement and partly because he didn't like seeing his neighbor naked. Shawn had made the most of the small dank basement, managing to bring in all sorts of abandoned alleyway furnishings in the form of various chairs and sofas that created quite the comfortable smoking room. It was a dingy drug house den. In the right state of mind it reminded him of opium dens he had seen in movies and TV shows, but in the light of day it just looked dirty.

"You want to come?" Shawn asked Ben as the punks began to descend the staircase.

"Nah man. I'll wait for Rina to get here." Ben answered back with a mouthful of Shawn's beans.

-

Outline of a dream:

We are in the desert. It is the desert but also seems familiar somehow. The ground is all red clay earth and it kicks up dust clouds whenever people walk over it. There are a few bushes and sparse grass. There is a small town that we are on the outskirts of. I am staying at some sort of school. The school is old and run down. There aren't many children in town so most of it remains unused. We have room in the basement. It is carpeted and there is one couch. I make a

bed on the floor. My friend Jon from high school is with me and he sleeps on the couch. Jon

brought a small guitar with him. He hasn't played it for me yet. He never played in high school.

There are two doctors in town. One rich, and one poor. The rich doctor treats all the white

patients in town while the poor doctor treats the Mexican immigrants and Indians who live

mostly outside of town. The next morning, Jon and I get to meet the poor doctor. We are outside

the school watching a group of young men and boys play soccer in the field next the school.

There is no grass and the red dust flies through the air in swirling spinning clouds. The doctor

tells us a story about the coyotes.

The coyotes are dying, and no one knows why. It seems he and the rich doctor used to be friends

many years ago. But they had a falling out over a research project they were both working on. He

didn't go into the details but he says he thinks he knows why the coyotes are dying.

The three of us go to town to the rich doctor's house. We meet his son who is a well built young

man. He works out constantly and is attempting to become a professional body builder. The poor

doctor confronts the rich one. The poor doctor starts to sweat profusely. His sweat comes out in

thick white droplets that run down over his face like maggots. It is disgusting to watch. The rich

doctor tells him to calm down and the sweat begins to run back up the poor doctor's face. The

maggot like droplets disappear back into the pores of his face. The dream ends.

-

The Nova punks were the punks that came from Nova. That is, Northern Virginia. They were, by

and large, harmless white kids from the suburbs of Washington DC that, as a general rule,

thought they were tougher than they actually were. This meant that they stayed out late

vandalized random objects, storefronts, the occasional car; and for the most part did a lot of drugs with ample allowances doled out on a monthly basis by their parents. The Nova punks were not a gang. There were entirely too many of them for that. They existed more like an ethnic group; bound together by similar interests and belief, or rather lack of, belief systems. They didn't all like each other. They didn't all know each other, but they were fairly easy for Ben to spot. Especially in the fall right before school started.

The big giveaway was their hygiene. The Nova punks always looked too well groomed. They were immaculate in their shining black leather and silver piercings. They had big smiles full of white teeth. Their dyed hair was too fresh and healthy looking. Their mohawks stood too high, betraying hours of effort to make them look just right. And though their mouths might spout profanity and talk tough their eyes still darted around constantly to reassure the owners that the act was going over swimmingly. The Nova punks were punks but they had purchased their cool with their parents' money and they had only just begun to live the lifestyle that their outward appearance so earnestly proclaimed.

Ben knew them all. Not personally but he knew them. He knew who they were. The world they were from. And he had partied with all of them. He didn't have anything against them. He just thought they looked so clean. He had seen their neighborhoods, those bright shining suburban palaces costing a quarter of a million dollars up north. It was amazing to him. Safe streets and secure family life hadn't kept these idiot kids from hating their parents and trying every drug under the sun. The Nova punks got out of high school after having spent all their free time roaming the streets of DC after hours, and now with their first taste of real freedom all they wanted to do was get high all day and wander the city in the sunlight exploring the streets and the back alleys for the filth and the garbage that anyone in their right mind would stay away from. Filth like Ben, and Shawn.

-

The Nova punks sat in the basement packing a bowl full of a schwag they had just bought from a mutual acquaintance Shawn had introduced them to. The re-sealable sandwich bag filled with an eighth of an once sat on the carpeted brick floor of the basement that predated all of current inhabitants of the building by at least eighty years. They sat planted on a couch that, like all the bits of furniture Shawn acquired, had seen better days. An old piece of reproduction furniture made to look like an antique settee. Its gold velour cushion had now faded to a dull yellow and the thick varnish on the wooden legs was cracked and peeling away. It was exactly the sort of thing Shawn loved. It was trash, but it was refined. It was garbage, cast away, and more than likely infested with a foulness that could never be cleaned or fumigated out. But it bespoke culture and sophistication and class. Or at least it once had. It was the finest piece of his garbage aesthetic and that was why it was in the smoking room.

 The smoking room. That was what Shawn called it in his not quite convincing accent. Shall we retire to the smoking room? He would ask as he entertained, he liked to call it entertaining, his guests. This was Shawn. The cultured aesthete sunk now to the lowest depths he could imagine, his well born background behind him, the decadence and depravity of the modern world surrounding him. He sunk into decay and rot and filth. He wallowed in it as if he was some glorious falling angel; fire streaming behind him from his flaming wings, falling to earth and sinking further to be reborn in the depths of hell.

 Shawn watched them pack the bowl, and stared into the burning cinders of the schwag as Jack took the first hit. The two of them together, Jack and Denny, mohawks arching backwards offered him the next hit. Shawn accepted trying to play the gracious host. He could afford better. Much better but he knew they'd take it as a slight if he didn't accept. He needed to accept in order to maintain his reputation. These two would bring others here. And as the new college year progressed Shawn's reputation would once again grow amongst the drug seeking freshmen. He truly enjoyed his position in the social hierarchy and he worked to maintain it. He imagined himself as a great purveyor of decadence. He looked forward to the coming school year.

 The Nova punks stared about in the dim light of the basement. There were no windows. Always a boon to the drug user who wished to hide their activities from prying eyes. In the darkness they could see that the basement extended much further but they couldn't discern how far. Beyond the light all they could see was dusty darkness and dirty brick. Shawn left them to finish their smoking, having been as gracious as he could, smoking their shit weed. But he was already stoned, and he wanted to see Rina. He knew she was here. He had heard her come in. I guess she still has the key, he thought to himself as he walked up the stairs from the basement listening to Ben's low mumbles in the kitchen.

6

"Hey baby. I brought you a sandwich." Rina said as she walked in through the back door of

Shawn's apartment. She scanned the room not seeing anything new or unexpected. She had first

hand knowledge of how Shawn lived. She used to stay here often enough.

"Oh damn. Thanks." Ben aroused from a light doze as Rina walked in the unlocked back door.

She might have knocked but he wouldn't have known it. Her head was cocked to one side and

backlit by the afternoon sun coming in through the window.

"I also got the robo. I got three just in case Shawn might want some." the sunlight silhouetted

Rina's thin frame drawing Ben's attention to her slim waist and attractive hips. He was a little

put off by the inclusion of Shawn in their little escapade for the evening. Ben hadn't really been

planning on tripping here at Shawn's but it was getting later and he needed Shawn to drive him

to the liquor store.

"Also good. "Ben reached out his hand for the sandwich Rina was pulling out of one of the

plastic bags she was carrying. "So what did you get me?" he asked as she placed the sandwich in

his hand.

"I got you an 'Italian sub'. " Rina answered back with a hint of playfulness in her voice.

"mmmm. I love Italians. " Ben teased back with a corny smile. "They taste so good with

mustard. "

"So let's do it.", Rina smiled at Ben's joke and pulled out two bottles of red cough syrup from

the second plastic bag she was carrying.

"Oh not yet. We should wait until tonight." Ben laid the sandwich across his lap and began to

unwrap it.

"Why tonight?" Rina sat down next to Ben slumping on the couch in Shawn's kitchen.

"I just like to trip at night. And I need to go to the store still. And it's too late in the day for a day trip. Which is what it would be if we started now. There are some rules you know." Ben was babbling and talking fast. He spread his hands wide in an exaggerated gesture that showed Rina just how stoned he was.

"Rules that you just made up. You're just stoned."

"Yeah."

"You're sharing that sandwich with me.", Rina said this and laid her head on Ben's shoulder.

"Ooh can I have some?" Shawn appeared from around the corner. The Nova punks were still in the basement.

"No way. ", Ben said with mock incredulity as he pretended to guard the sandwich with greedy hands.

"Man you just ate all my beans. You'd better share that with me.", Shawn's accented voice seemed to deepen into an almost forceful tone and even though Ben knew he was joking he didn't like it.

"Fine. But only if you can give me a ride." Ben handed Shawn half of the sub in his lap and gave the other half to Rina.

"But I don't want this whole thing." she interjected.

"Just eat what you want and I'll eat the rest." Ben patted her leg affectionately, almost paternally. He was, after all, nearly five years older than her.

"Where to?" Shawn asked through a mouthful of Italian sub sandwich. For all his 'English' affectations, he did not have very good manners.

"Liquor store, please." Ben replied, now acutely aware of not eating the sandwich they were all sharing between the two of them.

"Oh ho, big money day I see." Shawn said, assuming Ben had received his 'assistance check' for the month.

"No just a happy turn of events." Ben looked over at Rina munching away on the sandwich she had bought for both of them.

-

"Oh Jenny Jenny Jenny Faire, your red carpet of fiery hair has made me come alive and swoon, and still I lie here in your room, wishing ever infinitely, for yet another bite to eat, but what I'd really love to do, is yet again make love to you.", Berto read the words of his latest little poem to Jenny as she smiled conspiratorially at him. He was always making up little rhymes for her. He was always making up little rhymes for everyone and everything. It was nearly the only thing he did well. Jenny knew Berto wasn't a poet. He never studied poetry. He just liked the idea. And she just liked the idea of him.

She reclined back in her bed and pulled up her skirt revealing exactly that red carpet to which he had just composed his rhymes. She was chubby, and her thighs were no exception but the creamy white skin and pink flesh of her pubis excited Berto nonetheless.

The first naked women Berto had ever seen had been in pornographic films from the seventies. These films were purloined in secret from friends' fathers and distributed on a regular basis through a network of friends in a rotating cycle of masturbatory film appreciation. These women, with their full bushes of pubic hair and ample but natural bosoms stood in stark contrast to the tight tanned silicone filled women that were to dominate the pornographic films of Berto's later years. And it was in those later years, those more recent pornographic films, that Berto had noticed the shorn crotch. The tight little landing strip of pubic hair. A neatly trimmed garden rather than the wild jungle of femininity that Jenny displayed for him now. Berto mused over this as he delved into Jenny's thigh's face first to personally explore the jungle. Hot and steamy, moistening at his heated breath and gentle tongue. Berto loved the jungle.

-

"Whatcha doin?" lil Jim slurred the words out as he wiped the side of his face trying to remove the sticky partially dried drool from the indentations that had been left in his cheek by Fat Jenny's couch cushions.

"Nothing. Just watching TV." Berto answered the question without looking up from the TV. He and Jenny had thankfully finished their activities well before Jim woke up. Jim wasn't aware of Berto and Fat Jenny's new relationship and they wanted to keep it that way. "You passed out man."

"Yeah.", lil Jim replied. He sat down on the floor next to Berto who had his back leaned against the foot of Fat Jenny's bed.

"I told you not to smoke too much." Berto said to lil Jim though without condescension.

"Whatever." lil Jim shrugged off Berto's statement even though part of him appreciated the fact that Berto was trying to look out for him. "What time is it?"

"About seven… I am totally baked." Fat Jenny piped in from the bed with her head and hands resting on a pillow at the foot of the bed. Her voice floated down between Jim and Berto.

"What do you want to do tonight?" lil Jim asked. He and Berto hadn't been planning to do any thing specific but they had planned on hanging out together.

"I think I'm doing it." Berto answered back and lolled his head to the side toward lil Jim. Jim looked into Berto's red eyes and could tell that he and Jenny had been smoking more since Jim fell asleep.

"That's cool. Is it okay if we stay here?" lil Jim rolled his head back onto the top of the bed and could just barely see Jenny's eyes and the top of her head with its curly red hair.

"Sure. But you guys are doing the cooking and cleaning up.", Jenny was always making her houseguests clean so lil Jim expected this much. He was afraid that he might be doing all the cleaning up and cooking with the state that Berto seemed to be in.

"Sweet. You have cable right?" lil Jim asked Jenny.

"You know it." Fat Jenny pointed towards the cartoons that were scrolling across the small TV screen that faced the bed. Jim smiled and relaxed his back against the bed.

-

Outline of a Dream:

 I am moving. Well, not me, but some version of me. This is not my house and these are not my things but everyone treats them like they belong to me. There are movers milling around my house. They are looking for something to do. I haven't packed yet but I told them to come here on this day and here they are. They are ready to move things but I am not ready to move. They smirk and laugh at me behind my back. I can feel it. They are all big guys, sweaty. They look strong. They could probably beat me up in a fight. I am a little intimidated. They look at my girl friend. I don't have a girlfriend. I begin to realize that I am dreaming. I feel strangely aware that I am in two places at once. I feel the couch underneath me. The fabric of the couch cushions are rough on my face. Where am I? The dream ends.

-

Ben and Rina walked out back behind Shawn's apartment. They waited for Shawn to pull his car around from up the street and into the small parking lot behind his and the other apartment houses on the first block of Floyd Ave. There were ample parking spaces behind Shawn's apartment in the small gravel lot but Shawn had refused an offer of one when he moved in three years ago. It was, as he put it, better to not pay for parking and walk a little further. Shawn also liked to pocket the money that he would otherwise be paying for his parking space and use it to buy beer or a bag or whatever.

Shawn pulled the van in and in the waning sunlight Ben could see a few more dings and scratches along the side of the old Dodge caravan that Shawn drove. Shawn was a terrible car owner, he didn't change the oil regularly, he never washed the van and he wasn't particular about where he parked the van so it was often acquiring dents and scratches that had no explanation. The new dents would just show up, and Shawn would have no knowledge of how they got there. Ben couldn't drive at all, due to his left eye, which had been dysfunctional for as long as he could remember.

Shawn had been chauffeur to Ben's needs for as long as Ben had known Shawn, but to be fair Ben's needs were usually just being ferried to the liquor store and back. On rare occasions Ben would ask Shawn to take him out of the city.

The sun was still high in the sky and cast a glaring white light over everything in the lot. The burgundy Dodge seemed even dustier than normal and the light was highlighting the rust spots as Shawn pulled the van up to where Ben and Rina were standing in the gravel lot. A dust cloud floated gingerly behind it; kicked up by the wheels it floated forward and lightly enveloped the van as it stopped.

"Get in the front babe." Ben said to Rina as he grabbed the door handle to the large sliding panel door on the side of the van.

"You don't want shotgun?" she asked standing with the passenger side door open.

"No, I don't ever sit in the front seat." Ben said as he climbed into the back of the messy van.

There was only one long bench seat in the back. The second seat, normally standard on the Dodge Caravan had been removed and lost a long time ago; potentially adorning some other smoking room in some other part of the city. The remaining seat was secured in the far back of the van and created a great deal of distance between the driver and passengers in the back.

"Why don't you sit in the front?" Rina asked as she climbed into the passenger seat and pulled the door closed behind her.

Ben closed the big sliding door with a lurch forward that twisted his weight around in the van and shook it back and forth on its suspension creating a rocking motion. "Hey now, don't go a rockin." Shawn said in a corny voice even more strange due to its English character that neither Rina nor Ben responded to.

"Shawn won't let me ride in the front seat." Ben responded to Rina's question and slid backwards into the bench seat in the back.

"Why?" Rina looked at Shawn accusatorily.

"Because, if I am going to be his chauffer then his ass is going to ride in the back." Shawn's fake English accent softened the 'a' in ass, making it sound like 'ahhss' as he pointed backwards over his shoulder at Ben and gave a little fake laugh for emphasis as he pulled his van out the back parking lot.

Rina looked over her own shoulder at Ben who just shrugged as if to say 'that's just how Shawn is and you just have to accept it' and then looked out the window. He watched the indistinct shapes of the outside world float past him. Undetermined patches of color bordered and bled into each other as he squinted uselessly out of Shawn's van window. Ben was used to Shawn pushing him around and didn't think anything of it. Ben had been pushed around and made fun of for most of his life. His bad eye made him an easy target for bullies growing up. Shawn made fun of him but at least he wasn't always mean to him.

"Hey Shawn." Ben yelled towards the front seat.

"Yes?" Shawn said distractedly, his eyes darting from the rear-view mirror to the road and back again.

"Are those NOVA punks still in your basement?"

"Well yes, they are." Shawn laughed as he realized he had left the punks sitting in the basement smoking and hadn't told them where he was going or that they should leave.

7

Ben had learned to rely on the kindness of strangers, or at least their handouts. Every doctor who had ever examined him had pronounced him unfit for any kind of practical work and school had been all the more difficult. He was the living embodiment of that old adage: 'blind in one eye and can't hardly see out the other'. He had lived in foster care for most of the beginning of his life. When he turned eighteen he moved out onto the streets and finally wound up at a welfare office in the city.

He had managed to score a monthly disability check which was just enough to pay rent in a slum apartment and buy some food. Ben could barely read or see with what he referred to as his good eye and he had no practical skills. He had been living from check to check for the last eight years and spent most of his time high or drunk. His recent relationship with Rina had been the most exciting thing to happen to him for some time.

Ben traced his finger along the rubber seal of the window and the sill sitting in the backseat of the van. His arm extended and touching the window he bounced in the seat unsecured by the seatbelt in the bench seat that was designed to hold three people but rarely did. Shawn almost never chauffeured anyone. He didn't like the idea that people were taking advantage of him. But Ben knew he was a special case. Shawn genuinely liked him. Ben could feel that. Shawn was probably the only person Ben really trusted. Shawn was definitely the only person, besides the probing bastards down at social security, who knew exactly how little Ben could see with either eye. Ben was actually legally blind. Which is why he didn't drive. Shawn was the only person

Ben asked for anything from, and Shawn always obliged.

 Ben heard Rina laugh in the front seat. She was laughing at something Shawn said. The two of them were little more than blurry shapes to Ben sitting as far away from them as he was. He stared out the window, preferring the blurry shapes outside the van to the front seat and tried to ignore the fact that Shawn was flirting with Rina more now than before, when he was dating her himself.

-

 When the van returned to the gravel parking area behind Shawn's place Jack and Denny perked up from their perch on the pathetically small and run down concrete landing that Shawn's landlord graciously referred to as a back porch. Their respective mohawks glistened in the early fall sunlight with unknown ounces of hair gel and fixing sprays as Shawn parked his van illegally in the gravel lot. Jack smiled a big wide grin giving Shawn the impression that Jack was some kind of gargantuan toad; evil and squatting on the back stoop, waiting to devour whatever wandered into the path of his tongue. Jack's eyes drifted over Rina as she squirmed out of the van's front seat. He knew he would never be able to entice her into bed with him and it made him all the more lascivious. He stared. Rina ignored him. Ben came up behind Rina and only barely acknowledged Jack. Before anyone had even uttered a greeting Denny piped up,

"Where'd you go?"

"Store." Shawn answered without much enthusiasm and trying to not draw too much attention to the bottle of whiskey under his left arm though he could see Jack's eyes had moved on to staring lustily at something he could have. Fuckin' Nova punks, Shawn thought. All the fuckin' money in the world and they'll still try and beg something off you. Shawn didn't really care; he had 'all the fuckin' money in the world' too. Besides it wasn't his bottle anyway and Ben could share it with whoever he wanted.

"Liquor store huh?" Jack prodded knowingly directing the question at no one in particular.

"Yup." Ben mumbled back to no one in particular. The afternoon was gradually becoming evening and the shadows were getting long along the gravel parking strip behind the row houses where Shawn lived. Ben kicked at a small pocket of crabgrass that had staked its claim near the first step of Shawn's back stoop.

"You guys hanging out tonight?" Denny asked Ben as Rina began to squeeze between him and Jack who were sitting shoulder to shoulder on the stoop. Denny shifted a little but Jack moved not at all preferring to make Rina slide her leg along his shoulder as she moved up the stoop's two steps.

"Yeah, I guess." Shawn replied to Denny's question and walked up the steps towards the back door as well. Jack slid over for Shawn.

"What are you doin'?" Denny asked with a slow voice that Ben hadn't noticed until know. Denny's obvious high counterbalanced Jack seeming indifference to the weed they had just smoked in Shawn's basement.

"Tripping maybe. You want to hang out?" Ben asked knowing that if he did he was going to have to share his bottle with them.

"What's with the liquor then?" Jack asked starting to giggle at a joke only he understood. Ben felt like Jack was laughing at him but didn't bother saying anything.

"Why does everybody ask that?" Ben replied and followed Shawn and Rina inside to the kitchen with Jack and Denny trailing behind.

-

Outline of a dream:

I am dating a woman. She seems a little bit older. She is thin and has a few wrinkles on her face and dark curly hair that is wild and crazy. It sticks out in every direction as if she was always shaking her head back and forth violently. Despite her age she is incredibly sexy in a sheer silver dress that hangs just on the edges of her shoulders and has a very low cut back. She's not wearing a bra. We are standing in her apartment and everything is dark. The lights might be off. There is a little light coming in from the streetlights outside but it's a hazy unnatural neon kind of affair that only illuminates part of her face and leaves the rest in shadow.

 She takes me to the window and she wants to talk. She shows me the apartment across the street from her. I can see across the street and through the window directly opposite us I can see into a small apartment similar to hers. I see her standing over there looking back at me. Over in the apartment across the street she is different although she is dressed just the same. She is moving her head around wildly and she is laughing. It seems unhealthy. I look back at her standing next to me in the first apartment and she looks angry. She's angry with me. She is convinced that I am cheating on her with her double across the street. She's shaking her head around and angrily telling me to stop seeing her. She says she knows what I've been doing. I try to explain that she is just looking in a mirror and seeing her reflection across the street. She doesn't understand. She is crazy. I calm her down. The dream ends.

-

Ben suppressed his gag reflex as he swallowed the last of the sickeningly sweet cough medicine in Shawn's kitchen. He followed his last swallow with another swallow of his own saliva to try and get the taste out of his mouth. Shawn handed him a can of soda and Ben sipped it almost gingerly treading a fine line of nausea waiting for the sensation to pass. Rina and Shawn were still working on their bottles preferring to sip it all slowly rather than quaff it as quickly as possible. Ben preferred not to prolong his torture. Better to get a rush of nausea that comes and goes quickly than drag out the entire procedure. He sat down on Shawn's couch with a stomach full of gurgling red syrup and stared at the twenty year old TV set that sat less than two feet from the couch almost touching his knees. The back of the couch faced the back door of Shawn's apartment and the television was usually the first thing one saw as one entered the apartment. Afternoon cartoons danced and played tricks on each other across the screen. Ben only half paid it any attention. Rina slumped next to him and took a couple more sips from her bottle of cough syrup. Ben knew she probably wouldn't finish all of hers and then he would have to drink the rest which would lead to a better high for him. Shawn paced relentlessly across the floor of the kitchen.

"Where are they?" Shawn said as he sipped away at his bottle of cough syrup that was slowly turning his tongue a dull red. He turned the bottle up and lifted his little finger into the air in a mock gesture of daintiness.

"They'll come back." Ben replied to Shawn's rhetorical question. "What do you care anyway? You barely even like them." Ben didn't really care for them either but they often brought free weed to Shawn's so he couldn't complain.

"They're bringing my dinner back with them. I don't want to have to go out while I'm tripping. That would be ever so fucked up." Shawn, despite his reputation for being a social butterfly really hated leaving his apartment. He was a sort of social hub and people gravitated towards him even though he himself rarely liked actually doing anything. Unless he was fucking someone or had the potential to, then all the rules changed.

"Fucked up but fun." Ben knew Shawn didn't like going out when he was on anything but Ben kind of preferred it. He had spent some measure of time living alone and didn't like it at all. He felt reassured when people were around, knowing that if anything happened to him someone would likely help him or get someone who could. He had learned to rely on other peoples eyes especially when fucked up. That was why he at least liked going over to Shawn's place. There was always somebody there, even if only a couple of stupid NOVA punks.

"Yeah come on. I love going out when I'm tripping." Rina arched her back and stretched against Ben and yawned out the words as she said them. "It's so much more fun than sitting around doing nothing."

"Shit man. I just like tripping. I don't like dealing with the world." the words were truer than Shawn was willing to admit to. He didn't like dealing with the world. He never had though Ben wondered if Shawn had ever really *had* to deal with anything at all. At least not like Ben had.

"Whatever. Even if they don't come back, it's not like you paid them anything for dinner."

"They might also bring a girl or two with them." Shawn hadn't been laid in a while. He had been feeling horny for a couple of days but his prospects had been slim. He needed someone to bring some new meat into his little circle of acquaintances, hangers on, and generally lazy stoners. Ben smiled at Shawn as he finished off Rina's bottle and watched her curl up into a ball on Shawn's lumpy brown kitchen couch. Ben had slept here more times than he could remember. So had a lot of Shawn's friends. Ben was getting sleepy from the cough syrup and so was Rina.

"Those two losers aren't bringing any girls dude." He said finally as he half laid on top of her and nuzzled his face into the back of her neck.

"Not that fuck head Jack anyway. Did you see the way he was staring at me? He won't even look me in the eye; he just stares at my tits and my ass." Rina said lying on the couch with Ben's arm draped over her.

"You'd be singing a different tune if he wasn't such a fat fuck." Shawn laughed at himself and drained the last of his bottle as well. His accent always seemed to make his cursing seem more eloquent and refined than it actually was, even when he was being insulting. He settled into the remaining room at the foot of the couch with Ben and Rina's feet almost lying in his lap.

"What?" Rina started to wake up a little at Shawn's insult. She half rose up and kept Ben from falling into his traditional pre-trip nap. Ben usually fell asleep right before a robo-trip and so did Rina. It wasn't sleep really, just a sort half lucid daydream unreality that took over you for half an hour before the trip really began.

"I said you'd be singing a different tune if he wasn't such a fat fuck." Shawn stared straight ahead into the TV screen and stuck his chin up and forward giving his words an unconscious accentuation.. The fading sunlight coming in from the lone kitchen window lit up the back of his blond head making it seem as if he was haloed by a holy light. Rina wanted to kick him in the face.

"What the fuck does that mean?" Rina started to raise up even more into an almost sitting position. Ben tried to keep his arm around her but not move. He didn't want to wake up.

"I mean, the only reason you think he's a jerk-off is because you're not attracted to him. Jerk-off's father is probably rich. If that asswipe had a tight ass and the same size bank account you'd be all over his jerk-off ass. But then again so would every other skinny hot bitch in the tri-cities." Shawn had said jerk-off over and over again with an increasing emphasis every time. He even mouthed it to himself when he was done speaking though he never took his eyes away from the TV screen.

Ben's voice was muffled by the couch pillow he was shoving his face into to block out the light. "What does that even mean 'tri-cities'?" after he said this in an attempt to change the subject he tightened his arm around Rina's waist and pulled her back down to lay next to him. He really didn't like it when Rina and Shawn fought. They hadn't broken up so long ago that there wasn't still some animosity between them. If Ben wasn't Shawn's friend she probably would have never come back here.

"Fuck if I know. I heard it on the news I think." Shawn knew he had gone too far and looking over could see the anger in Rina's face. Damn he really needed to get laid. He knew Ben did too and Ben was really good to Rina but damn Shawn really needed to get laid. And Rina was so fucking hot. He was starting to get jealous. He turned his attention back to the late afternoon cartoons. This was the last one of the line-up; there would be sitcoms coming on next and that would be sufficient entertainment until the robo started to kick in.

Rina stared at the TV's colors and let the conversation drop, not wanting to continue with Shawn as long as Ben was around. She didn't want to make him choose between Shawn and her; partly for fear of who he might choose.

-

Outline of a dream:

I am with my father. Where is Mom? We are at his house. We are working on something but I don't know what. Maybe we are building something. Repairing something? Doing home improvements? Whatever it is there are power tools around and sawdust everywhere. There is also plastic sheeting but it is just lying about on the ground and seems torn and disorderly. No we are not in a house. We're in a building. It's almost completely empty. There's just trash everywhere. It looks like it's being renovated for something. The building is old. Dad needs my help. Where is Mom at? He says he needs me to help him do something. He's killed someone. He had to. They were going to kill him and he had no choice. But now there's this body and he needs me to help. We have to bury it. He needs me to help him bury this dead person and move on. The dream ends.

-

 Ben and Rina sat together in silence in the back room that served as a living room slash bedroom for Shawn's small apartment. Light from the kitchen trailed down the short hallway and into the dark bedroom. On the edge of Shawn's bed they both stared absently into the half lit darkness as the light played across random piles of clothing and pillows on the sparse carpeting. Ben tried to say something as he reached out and touched Rina's hand. She looked at him distractedly. She had had a thought just a moment ago. What was it? Something she needed to say. She couldn't remember now. Some new thought had immediately replaced before she get it out. Before she could make her mouth form the words she meant to say to Ben some new thought jumped into her head and kept her from talking. Kept her from speaking. No, it wasn't a new thought, it was a new...perception. She had noticed something. The bed. The bed was so stiff. The fabric felt like cardboard. Starchy. How did Shawn ever sleep here? How did she? She tried to look at Ben but got distracted again by the bed-sheet.

"You feel that?" she asked dazedly slurring the words as if she was speaking while she had glue in her mouth. Did she have glue in her mouth?

Ben touched her hand, his eye finding hers; he seemed to be wobbling while he sat there in front of her. "We're okay huh?" he asked more to reassure himself than to actually ask. He just needed to hear the sound of his own voice. He needed to talk. It took such an effort to speak. Just to focus long enough to speak to her. He saw a greenish haze around her ...on her. Her skin looked strangely green to him. He wanted her. He wanted to fuck her right there in Shawn's bed. What were they even doing here? How did they get here? Where was everyone else? They were all here just a moment ago. Weren't they? But now they were in the dark. Together.

Ben reached over and touched Rina's face. He turned her towards him again and away from the fascinating piles of clothing that had yet again grabbed her attention. He kissed her hard. Harder than he would if he wasn't tripping and forced his tongue into her mouth. Rina acquiesced willingly. Dazed as she was she still felt like her cunt was on fire. Ben pushed her back onto Shawn's bed and started to take off her shirt. Rina grabbed his shoulders and pushed hard sideways indicating that she wanted to be on top of him. She nearly tore his over-worn and threadbare pants as she undid his zipper and roughly sought out his dick. She was going to fuck him hard. Rina went down on Ben only for as long as it took to shimmy out of her own jeans and then she jumped on him not wanting to wait to get his cock inside her.

"Oh… fuck." Ben said as she slid him inside her pussy.

Ben and Rina didn't hear the floorboards of the old building creaking underneath Jack's feet as he slithered his bulk down the short hallway of Shawn's dingy apartment. He had come up to raid Shawn's fridge for the last of the ridiculously cheap twelve pack he and Denny had purchased on their dinner foray. Shawn and Denny were still in the basement getting higher and higher. Jack had heard the groans and muffled moans as soon as he opened the basement door. He smiled to himself as he had closed the basement door as quietly as possible behind him and watched Ben and Rina until they had finished and lay side by side naked on Shawn's bed. Jack slipped away as quietly as he had come delighting in the sight of Rina's naked form writhing in orgasm on top of Ben.

-

Outline of a dream:

Having sex. Making love. All I see is her body moving above me moving rhythmically. Breasts swaying, nipples moving in little circular motions. Barely noticeable circles. She is sighing, sort of grunting as she grinds into me. It feels good. Too good. I have to concentrate to not come too early. I close my eyes. All I feel is movement and flesh. Heat. I am sweating I start to feel thirsty. I feel the sheets like sand paper beneath my back. I close my eyes tighter and start to see red. Moving geometric shapes in little pixel-like patterns. All red. Red like blood red. There are little men in the blood. Little hairy men. Muscular demon men with dark hair all over their bodies. All in the blood. In her blood. I'm seeing into her blood! These men are working. Pushing and pulling grease laden gears as large as they are. Everything is covered in grease. Pistons. Gears. Levers. Up and down pushing and pulling in and out. Theses men are working. What are they working for? The orgasm. They're making her orgasm? They're driving towards it. Working harder for it. Faster. Sweating. Grinding. Screaming. Exploding relief. The dream ends.

8

Berto strolled leisurely down Harrison Street's ragged sidewalk. It wasn't what it used to be, not that Berto would know. He didn't know anything about the history of the neighborhood he lived in. Didn't matter anyway. It was early morning. About seven and none of the freshmen students unlucky enough to get stuck with early morning classes were out yet. It was nice to be out alone though the crisp air was already giving way to the muggy heat that was bringing in the day. He had left Fat Jenny's place less than half an hour ago for no reason other than he wanted to get out of there and away from lil Jim for awhile. Berto wasn't quite sure why he needed to get away he just did. He didn't want to get too close to Fat Jenny. He liked her enough but Berto definitely didn't want it getting around that he was diddling Fat Jenny on a regular basis. After all, what would people say about him fucking a fat girl? As long as he managed to keep his visits to Jenny's boudoir infrequent he could keep her from trying to make it a steady thing between them.

He had slipped out of bed quietly enough, and had remembered not to step on the floorboard right outside her room that would have creaked loudly enough to wake both her and lil Jim. Lil Jim was snoring away on Fat Jenny's couch as Berto closed the front door to the apartment and casually walked down the four flights of stairs to Grove Street. Big wide concrete sidewalks had greeted him in his black, scuffed boots. He had walked four blocks to Harrison and taken a right, walking now on a torn brick surface that nearly tripped him every few steps when he wasn't looking. He was meandering towards the 7-11 at the corner of Main Street.

Berto fumbled in his front left pocket for the remainder of his cigarettes and found one. It was nearly flat with a vicious fold half an inch from the brown paper filter. As he kept walking on Harrison Street's red brick sidewalk he gently straightened it and placed the brown filter between his lips. He dug deeper in his pocket for the pink lighter he had accidentally stolen from Fat Jenny. To spite her bulk Fat Jenny liked to surround herself with bright colors. To draw attention to herself this need trickled down even to the accoutrements and trappings of her smoking paraphernalia. The little lighter, which seemed all the more dainty in Fat Jenny's chubby fingers, was bespecked with tiny blue flowers on a field of pink. It was no exception to Fat Jenny's need for color. It seemed to scream: "I am a girl" at Berto and the rest of the world. He snapped down his thumb turning the little grinding wheel against the flint inside and igniting the butane flame. Touching the flame to the end of the cigarette in his mouth and cupping his hand around them both to keep the flame from going out he inhaled deeply. He pulled in as much smoke as he could and held it in as he looked up at the blue morning sky. He exhaled slowly and nearly tripped again as he stepped hard into a hole in the walkway. There were several bricks missing here. Berto looked around to see if anybody noticed his slip. He was nearly alone. No one looked his way. He kept walking to the convenience store.

-

Shawn had woken up confused and tangled in the suspiciously stained sheets of his small bed. Jack and Denny had left soon after their beer had been depleted and Shawn had no idea what time Ben and Rina had let out as he found himself alone and groggily shifting in his bed. A golden morning light streamed in from the one window in his bedroom casting a sanctifying glow over everything it touched. He lay on his back not wanting to move and utterly refusing to acknowledge his own conscious state as he stared at the minuscule particles of dust floating and dancing through the shafts of warm light entering through the window. The dust spun and traveled in jerky purposeless paths in every direction as Shawn half dreamed that if he could only managed to figure out why these particles moved the way they did he would know all the secrets of the universe. He closed his eyes again in an attempt to regain unconsciousness.

The window which faced a small recessed area between the two row houses was even more dirty and piled with cast off garbage than the rest of the parking lot behind Floyd Avenue. The grass which only managed a small purchase elsewhere in the lot grew long and wild in the back of the little recess under Shawn's window bringing to mind images of creeping insects that might bite and itch and were all the more monstrous and unclean because they lived in the depths of a city rather than out in the forest where they belonged. Shawn could never bring himself to walk back into the recess between the houses due largely to his inability to drive the image of tiny microscopic biting mites from his mind whenever he looked at the tall grass.

He finally lost the interior battle he was fighting with the mind that patently refused to re-enter the peaceful dream world where he had been enjoying his temporary amnesia only minutes before and swung his legs out of bed and let his feet touch the floor. The morning light had illuminated everything in the room and was glaring fitfully off of a white business sized envelope on one of the few empty patches of floor. Shawn recognized it as a letter he had noticed yesterday that was hand addressed in his father's handwriting. He had forgotten about it until now.

Shawn groaned as he stood up and felt the cold rush of a temporary blackout coming on. He had stood up too quickly and the subsequent loss of blood pressure made him dizzy as a gold pixilated patterning took over his vision. He had always wondered why people always referred to this sensation as blacking out. He never saw black. He always saw this gold color pattern. This shifting pixel pattern that bled in from the sides of his vision and completely obscured everything for ten or twelve seconds as his body made the adjustment from sitting to standing too quickly. The blackout passed and his vision cleared as Shawn moved confidently if less than gracefully across the littered room towards the white envelope. He inserted a finger under a space in the back flap and tore the envelope open to read the contents of the brief letter. His eyes widened and his shoulders slumped the weight of the realization that his father was tired of his uncommitted and infrequent enrollment at school, his poor performance and his general lack of direction in life. His parents were cutting him off. They were not exactly wealthy, but they were well off enough and had managed to support him fully for several years. The dream was over. Shawn was shocked. What the fuck was he going to do?

-

Berto sat outside the convenience store on Main and Harrison and waited. He occasionally glanced over his shoulder at the entrance to check the ashcan next to the door. The traffic roared by deafeningly in a consistent drowning drone of noise that would have impeded any conversation Berto would have engaged in if he wasn't alone. He had made the rounds once already and was now just waiting. He had come by here first, looking for discarded butts in the sand filled ash cans outside the entrance to the tiny convenience store that held more nicotine laden tobacco than Berto could smoke in a lifetime. It was all just out of his economic reach. His first round was a bust. He had come by too early and too late. He was too early for enough customers to have been by and stubbed out a good butt in the can, but too late to gather butts from the night before. By the time Berto had arrived, the morning shift had already cleaned the cans and the only butt in them was already useless as it had been smoked down to the filter. After his first visit to the store entrance Berto immediately veered off in the direction of campus just across the street. Most of the entrances to the campus Business school had ash cans outside and Berto made a visit to each one. He was again too early but checking them all had resulted in one decent butt; there was about a quarter of a cigarette left and he pocketed it as quickly as he could looking around to see if any one saw him. This would be harder to do later in the day, and he had to swallow his fragile pride on several occasions when there were too many people around for him to grab butts with out anyone seeing. He didn't like anyone seeing but most times he didn't have a choice. The best butts came in the middle of the day when the most people were on campus to deposit them.

The best cigarette butt was only partially smoked and stubbed out straight and clean in the sand. These were ideal, but especially rare; although the Business school was the best place to find them. The Business Building catered mostly to general education courses and commuter students. People with jobs and a little money that were in a hurry to get in and out of class. Not like the art building on the other side of school where every art student scrounged for money and smoked every cigarette down to its bitter toxic filter as if the act of smoking itself were a religious rite. Every cigarette, every time.

The worst butts were those with enough tobacco left to be irresistible but with a little repugnant lipstick stain on the filter. Berto's stomach always turned a little as he smoked them and the lipstick's image hovered in his mind as a sticky reminder of the butts' former owners. Sloppy seconds of the highest order. He always tore the filter in half and removed the interior 'filter fuzz' as he liked to call it. Berto did this with every butt he found. Doing this left just enough paper to hold onto, and made the whole nicotine fix stronger as there was no filter left to inhibit the smoke. But that lipstick would still bother him. He didn't like to be reminded of what he was doing anymore than he liked anyone to see him scrounge for the found butts in the first place.

But he had to what he had to do. And now he was waiting.

-

"What the fuck am I going to do?" Shawn stared into the rear-view mirror to see Ben's distracted gaze squinting back at him. Ben was situated in the center of the back seat of the van. Bits of tissue rolled past crushed paper bags emblazoned with colorful logos that once held fast-food while empty plastic soda bottles careened about the cavernous space between them making muted popping sounds every time they collided with each other.

"I dunno, what do you want to do?" Ben responded loudly so Shawn could hear as he stared forward blurrily.

"I don't know what to do. I just can't believe they are cutting me off. It's mostly my father. My mother would never hang me out like this. Dad has always thought I was an irresponsible idiot."

"Well, aren't you?" Ben jokingly retorted. "You could get a job, I guess."

"What, sling coffee and drinks down at the Village?" Shawn turned the van to the right and two empty soda bottles bounced over Ben's feet.

"Shit man, you'd be lucky to get a job at the Village, those guys make good money." Ben couldn't tell where they were anymore. They had pulled out of Shawn's place ten minutes ago and he had stopped paying attention but he trusted Shawn not to get them lost.

"I've never done anything like that before." Shawn sounded pathetic as he let out the words; Ben knew that Shawn had never really done any work in his life. Not that Ben felt like he had either. "I don't think they'll hire me."

"Probably right. What have you done before?"

"Nothing really. I worked at a fast-food place in high school, and then briefly again when I started school." Ben noticed that Shawn's fake accent was slipping a little as he talked about his past; the time before he had acquired it. Shawn had always been a strange duck as far as Ben was concerned. Ben knew almost nothing about him other than he seemed to come from some serious money and never had to really worry about a thing as long as Ben had known him. The privilege Shawn came from had afforded him everything he wanted and thus seemed to take all drive and direction out of him. Shawn didn't really do anything. It had made him a perfect companion for Ben who, due to his long standing disability, couldn't do anything at all. "But I quit a long time ago." Shawn said.

"What have you done since then?" Ben asked but he knew the answer.

"Nothing."

"So, you haven't had a job since you were in high school? How long have you been out?" Ben had never quite gotten a straight answer to this question from Shawn though he had asked several times. Ben didn't know Shawn's real age but he had guessed he was in his mid to late twenties just like him; old enough to impress the younger freshman girls but not too old to scare them off. "Awhile." Shawn gave his typical non-committal answer implying with the exasperated tone of his voice that he was already older than the hills two hours to the west of their fair city dwelling. The hills they were presently heading towards in the van.

"And you still don't have your degree?" Ben prodded Shawn knowing that Shawn always took some classes just to keep up the pretense that he was pursuing a career path in good faith. Ben also knew that Shawn took classes so he would have something to talk to his parents about during the weekly phone calls that Shawn had come to dread even though he was often too high to remember them exactly.

Shawn turned the van to the right again and started to accelerate. "What fucking degree?" he said glancing in the mirror. "I've changed my major so many times and I barely pass my classes when I do take them. I haven't even been a full-time student for a year. What am I possibly qualified to do?"

"Nothing man. Just like me." Ben smiled at himself and his own ineptitude not knowing if Shawn was looking and incapable of seeing if he was.

"Indeed." Shawn's overly formal speech laced with its modest not-quite-english-but-somewhat-english-nonetheless-accent was beginning to return.

"I suppose you could move in with me; if you don't mind living in a shithole." Ben finally offered what Shawn had been fishing for all morning with the offer to drive Ben out to the mountains for a short hike. It was Friday and Shawn didn't have classes so it was an easy gesture of friendship and a good excuse to give them some time to talk. It was a gesture he was sure would pay off but knew he needed to go through the motions to get the offer out of Ben. Shawn could live for three months on the money he had left if only he didn't have to pay rent on his apartment. And he knew Ben would be a pal and let him move in; things were looking up.

"Look around you. Does it look like I would mind?" Shawn upturned his hand and gestured to the interior of the van with a little circular motion that Ben failed to appreciate fully from his vantage in the back seat. Ben caught the jist of what Shawn was trying to illustrate as his attention was re-drawn to the rolling tumbleweeds of trash around his ankles. He nodded, feeling as if he was one step behind the conversation. It was difficult when people talked with their hands.

"What will you do for money?" he asked.

Shawn smiled; he had no intention of getting a job now that Ben had come through. "I have a little, so that will do for awhile. And then I suppose I can do what you do."

"Nobody wants to do what I do." Ben replied staring out the window of the van. The landscape was slowly turning green and blue in contrast to the formerly ominous gray blur of the city; he sighed lightly feeling relaxed and said in a too low for Shawn to hear, "Not even me."

-

"You're going to let him move in?" Rina stared at Ben with dark eyes that from across the distance of the bed seemed black and beady and full of spite. "Here?" she said throwing an arm out to indicate the smelly digs of Ben's tiny hovel that Rina only infrequently visited. Ben didn't really believe that his apartment was nice enough to entertain in but the lowered rent allowed him the luxuries of some beer money and an occasional bag. It was enough for him but would was clearly too small for the addition of Shawn.

"Yeah." Ben replied in a low monotone not wanting to engage in this discussion with Rina. He squinted at her in her underwear.

Rina sat down on the bed and leaned in a little so that her face would be more in focus. She had begun to learn the boundaries of Ben's perceptions better and better over the past few weeks. "Don't you think that will be weird? I mean with the three of us?" Rina referred to her history with Shawn with a knowing tone hoping that Ben would get the hint.

"I'm not asking you to date him again." Ben said flatly and not wanting to argue. "He just needs a place to stay and I have room. His father's cutting off his money supply. Plus, you don't even live here." Ben's back was resting against the headboard of his bed. The frame creaked underneath his weight as he adjusted and squirmed slightly under Rina's inquisitive stare. His naked body was covered to his crotch by sheets that he hadn't washed in two months; he had hardly slept here since he had hooked up with Rina.

"Oh boo hoo poor Shawn won't be getting his thousand dollars a month to live on anymore. So he might actually have to learn to do something with his life now."

Rina mocked Shawn's predicament. And Ben didn't appreciate having to defend Shawn's self imposed financial hardships. "Easy, bitter." he said, hoping that would be the end of it.

"Whatever.", Rina said realizing she was being hard on Ben for the things she didn't like about Shawn. "I know he's your friend but he's kind of an asshole."

"I just want to help him. And where is all this hostility coming from? You guys were getting along fine the other day in the van." Ben decided to turn the conversation back on itself and resolve some of the residual jealousy he was still feeling about Shawn and Rina. As much as Ben liked Shawn it irked him to no end when Shawn flirted with Rina.

"He can be funny," Rina said nonchalantly, "but that doesn't make him any less an asshole. Why are you so nice to him?"

"Because he's good to me."

"No he's not, he makes you sit in the back of his van when he drives you around and he's always teasing you and shit..." Rina raised her voice a little, sat back and stared at Ben with incredulous eyes. The bed creaked loudly as she withdrew just out of Ben's focus.

"He doesn't mean it when he teases me. You wouldn't understand, all right?" Ben reached forward and touched Rina's hand. She looked at him gently and could feel herself feeling uncomfortably sorry for Ben. He was too forgiving of Shawn. "Shawn's been my friend for so long." Ben continued. "It's not the same when he makes fun of how blind I am. Look, he won't mess with us. I know you don't like him. You and I will just stay at your house more often. You don't even like it here anyway." As true as that was, Rina couldn't help but feel that Shawn would find a way to interfere with them. She didn't trust him.

"Fine." she said.

9

Berto hefted the aged television from Shawn's apartment with noticeable distress. The assembled friends and acquaintances of Shawn, and vicariously Ben, glanced in his direction with mild concern as he waddled his way forward towards the stairs of Ben's apartment building. The long cord which Berto had casually bundled up in his left hand as he had picked up the TV from Fat Jenny's trunk slipped from his grasp as he meandered forward and gave everyone including Shawn the impression that he might at any moment trip.

"You want help with that?" Shawn asked.

"Nah…hhmmph." Berto answered back as he jerkily adjusted his grip again.

"Don't break it strong-man." Fat Jenny said to Berto's back as he walked away. Berto had a penchant for trying to impress in not-so-subtle ways that seemed comically tragic to Fat Jenny. She knew he liked to think of himself as strong and capable and she liked to stroke his ego to make him feel good about himself. She had, on many occasions come back into her bedroom carrying a late night snack to find him standing in front of the mirror sucking in his flabby but small belly and puffing out his mostly hairless and pasty chest. She assumed the mirror revealed to Berto not his actual appearance, which she did admire but would never in any way describe as physically fit, but instead some distant future self that only Berto could see or believe in. Berto didn't see himself. He only saw what he believed in, what he believed himself to be. Or perhaps what he believed he could convince everyone else to see. That was why he had opted for carrying the heaviest of Shawn's items and objects by himself. He couldn't show off if he was just assisting someone move some big piece of furniture. As he huffed up the narrow, stinking staircase to Ben's second floor one bedroom the assembled movers stood aside on landings and in doorways offering assistance that was not appreciated.

Though most of Shawn' furniture had been laid gingerly next to the trash dumpsters across the gravel lot behind his apartment, he had kept his bed including mattress and box-spring which he and Ben dragged out of the back of his van. Ben struggled for a hand hold as Shawn pulled the awkward mattress too quickly. "Hey, not too fast." Ben said catching the soft cloth behemoth at the last possible instant.

"We're moving. The sooner we finish the sooner we drink." Shawn said and did nothing to slow his gait as he almost pulled Ben behind him with the heavy load. He wanted to get this over with. He wasn't anxious to live with Ben or anything but he hated doing any kind of physical activity and he was anxious to get the party started. Fat Jenny had brought some killer weed and a new friend who had come by only on the condition that she not be required to lift anything heavy. Shawn smiled at her as he lumbered past her slightly chubby but cute face. Her dark hair was cut into a bob and sported a tacky braided rat tail that hung over her left shoulder. She had come to his moving party wearing black and white striped tights black lipstick and a pair of dark polished and more than likely new oxblood boots. Yeah she was cute alright, and Shawn couldn't help showing off in front of her and bossing everyone else around.

"Right. Do you think Jack and Denny are coming by?" Ben said though he hoped not.

"Nah. They won't come by for at least a few days. That way they don't have to even think about helping me to move." Shawn retorted, looking over at the new girl to see if she was looking at him. She was. "I'm sure all of these guys will be hanging out though." Shawn cocked his head towards the group of friends who had actually showed up on his moving day as he started backing up the stairs. Most of them, Berto and lil Jim especially, had only shown up for the free beer and pizza Shawn had offered for their help. It was a last hurrah before his father finally stopped the money flow. Fat Jenny had come to be near Berto and smoke pot with Shawn. Rina had come because it was Ben's place and she felt like she ought to. Judy, the new girl whose slight belly was creeping out from beneath her short black shirt, didn't know why she was here but she carried some of the lighter boxes up the stairs anyway. Standing behind Ben she stole glances past him at Shawn. She did think he was cute, though. Maybe coming today would be worth it after all.

-

Outline of a dream:

 I am walking down Grace Street, or whatever amounts to Grace Street. It's more like a memory of Grace than it is actually Grace. It's a conglomeration of sounds and sights, blurry impressions that all bundle together but somehow end up reforming into the general impression of Grace Street. Anyway I think that it's Grace Street. On the corner is the storefront that has always been empty. For the life of me I can't remember anything ever being in there. I've always loved the stained glass windows along the side facing Harrison but I've never really looked closely at them from the street; only stared at them from the booths at the Village across the way. "Away and a way.", that's what D used to say. She used to live just down the street from here, two floors above me and dreaming of a better life. I think she finally found it, though I never understood what was so wrong with the life she had. Sure the furniture was old and looked like it came from one of those discount warehouses where you buy reject floor models that haven't been in style for years but it was mostly comfortable and plush and she used to fall asleep on that hideous couch every night watching old reruns on cable. I think they comforted her. They made it easier to ignore the terror of sleeping and possibly having another bad dream. Another dream about the world coming to an end. She did have a rough time there for awhile.

I don't look around the street. I don't look up or down I just move forward almost floating. Everything at the edge of my vision is hazy and blurry, and I know this is a dream but I let it go anyway. It just pulls me along with it as if I, the originator of the dream itself, have little to do with the direction at all. I try not to think to hard about the fact that I'm dreaming or else I might just wake up by accident. It feels so good to be dreaming. I go in a store. I go inside that old crappy magazine and stationary store next to the crappy Chinese place where all the punks used to hang out on Saturday nights eating egg rolls and General Tsao's, greasy and dripping with duck sauce over pork fried rice. Damn I miss that stuff.

The store is full of random racks of paper and magazines only old men would want. Golf, sport fishing, pornography. I remember this store. I came in here once a long time ago. They sell American Spirit cigarettes cheaper than anybody else on this street. I hate American Spirit cigarettes but everyone I know always wants me to smoke them because they are 'all natural'. I don't care. I prefer the trace amounts of arsenic in my nicotine. It tastes better.

There's porn in the back. Lots of porn. I came here with someone. A long time ago. A long time ago. I made a mental note of this store so I would remember to come back to get a porno mag when my friend wasn't with me. I didn't want him to know.

I see the old man behind the counter. There's something wrong with him but I can't put my finger on it and decide I'd prefer not to. Whatever afflicts him can just as soon remain his business and his alone. I don't want to know him or anything about his bald head and blue shirt and yellow cardigan. One side of his mouth drops down in a sickening point. He smiles a crooked droopy missing tooth smile. The dream ends.

-

Ben's apartment didn't feel as dingy once you were in it, and drunk. Once drunk it was easy enough to ignore the hole in the wall behind the stove and the thick carpet of grime in the corners of the bathroom's tile floor. It became progressively easier to ignore the eggshell walls painted in thick coats of a latex semi-gloss that was beginning to brown at the corners of the ceiling where the smoke from a thousand cigarettes and a hundred thousand bong hits and bowl packings. Every floorboard creaked under Ben's weight as he crossed the small living room into the kitchen where the meager green refrigerator, that matched the ancient brown gas stove next to it in age only, held a case of Milwaukee's Best. The cheap linoleum in the kitchen peeled up where it met the hardwood floorboards of the rest of the apartment. It provided a nice spot for dust and dirt from the outside streets of Richmond to collect; telling its own secret story of endless days of wandering and blowing on the wind, crumbling brick, cigarette ash, and decay. The detritus of Ben's days upon days gathered together to write a private history that no one would read.

"Anybody need one?" Ben called out to the moving crew assembled and sprawled on the old couches in the living room.

"Sure." an indeterminate number of voices called back.

"How many?" Ben asked in return unable to correctly assess the number of people in his living room requiring refills. It was the unwritten law of beer retrieval etiquette; if he went to the refrigerator for his own refill he was obliged to offer to bring one for someone else.

"Just bring em all." Shawn called out above the din of voices laughing, giggling and alternately calling out for beers.

"Sure.", Ben said to himself more than anyone else. He talked only to hear himself in the kitchen. The apartment was so often empty that it felt strange to him to be hearing a cacophony of voices in his own living room. His apartment suddenly didn't feel like his own anymore. It felt like…Shawn's place.

"Do we need to go out and get more?" Berto asked hopefully, wanting to go for a walk and feeling like he could still reasonably get a few more free beers out of Shawn.

"In a bit. In a bit." Shawn answered noncommittally watching Ben re-enter the room with the remainders of the case. Ben dangled it easily with one hand and Shawn could tell it was light. They would need to go for more. And probably soon.

Lil Jim swung in close to Shawn's ear and made a strange sound. "Wonna wonna wonna." Shawn had his back angled towards lil Jim and so he could keep his eyes on his left and on New Girl Judy. Her dark lipstick was all he could see of her face but her thigh rested against his in a flirtatious touch. The sound coming in his right ear irritated him and he jerked quickly around. "Man fucking stop that." Shawn said forcefully looking into lil Jim's red eyes.

"Sorry." lil Jim said insincerely. He wasn't sorry. He had drifted off into his own stoned world. Where his thoughts raced as he dazedly stared around his circle of friends. They laughed and joked with each other seemingly not as affected by the amounts of beer and marijuana they'd ingested that evening. "What are you doing?" lil Jim called out to Berto who was sitting on the floor next to Fat Jenny with his head down and focused on a notebook in his lap. Berto said nothing, supposedly not hearing lil Jim.

"What are you doing?" lil Jim said it louder this time causing the conversations between Ben and Rina and Shawn and New Girl Judy to cease momentarily as they stared at him. He leaned forward awkwardly in his seat on the couch next to Shawn. Lil Jim stared at Berto.

"Nothing." Berto's attention shot back to his notebook as he self-consciously covered it up with his left hand. "Nothing, really." he said again nonchalantly.

"He's writing a poem." Fat Jenny finally said in response to lil Jim's blank drooping stare.

"No I'm not." Berto said stealing glances towards Shawn and the others though their interest had already returned to each other.

"Yes you are. Can I read it?" Fat Jenny continued in teasing tone of voice nudging Berto gently in the side as they sat on the floor together. She flirted with him gently and no one paid them much attention. "Is it about me?" She asked with a low breathy voice that at once made Berto uncomfortable and excited. She was violating the unwritten rules of their non-relationship.

"It's not about anything." he said finally in answer to her probing and flirtatious prodding.

"What's it about?" lil Jim finally interjected with a tone of voice that was utterly inappropriate for his distance across the small circle of the living room.

"It's not about anything really." Berto replied to lil Jim promptly this time knowing that if he didn't lil Jim's voice would just get louder and louder until someone answered him or yelled at him to stop. Lil Jim looked away swaying his drunk and stoned gaze about the room haphazardly. He was bored with the conversation but had still felt a need to be part of it. Most of all he just hated being ignored by Berto when there were so many people around. Lil Jim felt left out of everything; and everyone had someone to talk to but him.

"Everything's about something." Shawn looked Berto and Fat Jenny alternately in the eye. He had been paying a half interested attention to them both as he tried to woo New Girl Judy who shifted a little on the couch next to him creating a light swooshing noise as her slightly chubby thighs rubbed her stockings together.

"Well. I mean, it is about something," Berto slurred his speech a little as the beer was beginning to take its toll on his communicative ability. "but it's hard to explain."

"Thanks." Shawn said to Ben who had started distributing the last few beers in the open case he had sat in the middle of the living room floor earlier.

"Thanks."

"Thanks." Fat Jenny said as Ben handed her the last beer and shook the case to indicate to everyone that it was finally, irrevocably empty.

"Wonna wonna wonna." lil Jim leaned in and made his stoned noise in Shawn's ear again.

"Jesus!" said Shawn jumping in his seat and disturbing the rickety couch. "Stop that you annoying little fuck." Shawn said as calmly as he could. Lil Jim was clearly annoying him. Why couldn't he just sit there and keep his stupid stoner sound effects to himself?

"Sorry.", lil Jim giggled to himself, clearly not feeling apologetic.

"Here.", Fat Jenny handed lil Jim the last beer that Ben had given to her. She hoped that would calm him down and he would stop annoying Shawn or at least get off the couch.

"So what are you going to do now?" New Girl Judy said to Shawn making small talk as she let her thigh rest against his again as he resettled into his seat.

"I don't know. I'm still trying to adjust to having no money right now." Shawn answered back

"So how much was your momanddad giving you?" Berto asked in bad taste.

"Not much. Not much." Shawn tried, as often as he could, to never answer this question directly if he could avoid it. His parents' money too often inspired envy in his friends and acquaintances. The less they knew about the specific amounts, the better.

"That's a fucking lie." Rina piped in from the other side of Ben on the small couch. She knew more than the others did as to the exact amounts he received from his parents to support himself, much to his dismay. "He was getting like a thousand a month to live on."

"Really?" Fat Jenny asked incredulously. She stared at Shawn, usually comfortable being the center of attention, now rather embarrassed and slouching in the couch under the weight of the judgmental stares.

"About that." Shawn said without much affect or accent.

"Did you save any of it?" Fat Jenny asked.

"No."

"Where the fuck did it all go?" Berto cussed for emphasis much of the time although the words never sounded quite comfortable coming out of his mouth. Despite the fact that he was at least as old as Fat Jenny and Rina, Berto always gave the impression of a school boy cussing outside class, looking over his shoulder to see if any teachers heard him.

"I don't know, probably lost it all on gas ferrying his ass around all the time." Shawn gestured towards Ben trying to shift the subject from his finances.

Ben rolled his eye at Shawn's implication and smiled a stubbled grimace at Rina who rubbed his shoulder in a conspiratorial fashion. "Whatever."

"Wonna wonnna wonna." Lil Jim started in on Shawn again, drawing his attention away from Ben and Rina.

"Fuck it.", Shawn said as he pushed lil Jim off the couch. Lil Jim landed laughing to himself and spilling his beer on the carpet flecked with bits of tiny stone and bread crumbs. "I fucking warned you lil Jim. I fucking warned you." Shawn said as he scooted his ass back into the corner that lil Jim had been sitting in on the couch.

"You really mean you didn't save any of it. Nothing at all?" New Girl Judy glanced down at lil Jim as if nothing had happened as Fat Jenny asked Shawn the question. Lil Jim sat up shakily and continued drinking what was left of his beer.

"Nothing. Well a little. Enough to live on for awhile." Shawn answered back.

"Are you gonna get a job?" New Girl Judy asked.

"Not if I can help it."

"What do you want to do?" Fat Jenny asked.

"Nothing." Shawn answered meaning it. He truly wanted to do nothing. He had lived the last few years with absolutely no ambition at all and it had pleased him endlessly. This was all he wanted. In his heart, he knew he wanted to do nothing. He wanted no responsibility, no attachments, and no obligations.

"What would you do if you could do anything?" New Girl Judy asked, her purple eyes glossing over with a willful and dreamy indifference that refused to acknowledge anything about the unexpected limitations of real life.

"Like I said… nothing. What about you?" Shawn said feeling stuck in a circle of stoners talking about dreams that would never come true.

"I'd build a huge statue of myself and put it out on Monument Ave." Berto interjected himself back into the conversation, despite the fact that the question had been addressed to new girl Judy. He had put his notebook down, presumably done with whatever he had been doing. "Wouldn't that be fucked up? A ridiculous statue of me with all those civil war heroes."

"Yeah, you should put yourself on a horse too." Lil Jim said.

"Nah. You should be a horse. Like your face on a horse's body." New Girl Judy giggled with delight at the thought of Berto's head , or anyone's head, on a horses body in the middle of that ridiculous avenue of nineteenth century monuments. Fat Jenny made a fake neigh in response to New Girl Judy's laughter.

"I'd pay for school and get myself out of debt before I graduate." Rina said.

"Are you still in school?" Shawn asked.

"Yeah Shawn, some of us actually do go to our classes and pass." Rina mocked him.

"Amazing. You mean you're not a drop out like myself?" Shawn mocked back.

"No, amazingly enough I am not."

"I'd buy a farm." Ben said with a quiet honesty.

"What?" Shawn looked at Ben surprised.

"I'd buy a farm. Way out in the middle of nowhere. Raise goats or something." Ben repeated.

"How the hell are you going to run a farm?" Shawn said insensitively drawing attention to Ben's disability.

"Not like I'll ever be able to afford it." Ben shrugged off Shawn's allusion and leaned back against the couch staring at the ceiling.

"Why do you want to live on a farm man?" Berto asked.

"It'd be nice to wake up every day listening to birds or something instead of fucking cars or construction equipment all the time. You know, smell grass occasionally."

"So that's why you want to live on a farm? Just so you can hear birds?" Shawn asked.

"That's not just it. I mean, I've lived in cities or suburbia like my whole life. And it is never quiet. I think it would be nice to go somewhere that I didn't have to listen to some stupid machine buzzing all the time. You know just get away from everything and live on my own."

"Can I live on your farm baby?" Rina asked rubbing Ben's belly full of beer and pizza.

"Yeah me too." Fat Jenny said.

"Sure. You all can." Ben smiled at the thought of all of them living together, but he was acutely aware that it would never happen. Fat Jenny would finish her art degree and start teaching somewhere in the suburbs. There was no telling how long Berto would stay in the city, but he was bound to get his shit together at some point and leave. Rina was just as likely to get bored with him as keep dating him for another few months. Besides all this, Ben was never going to have enough money to move anywhere but up and down the block from cheap apartment to cheap apartment.

"Do you think we'll be able to order pizza on the farm?" lil Jim asked Ben, taking the fantasy further in his head as he had sat there quietly sipping his last beer. Ben had thought he was asleep sitting up.

"I doubt it." Ben said raising his head off the back of the couch to look at lil Jim.

"Then I can't come." lil Jim said with a sad honesty.

"Well nobody thought you'd be going anyway." Shawn said meanly wanting to pick on lil Jim to pay him back for annoying him earlier.

"Can't we all come?" Fat Jenny said partly to smooth things over between Shawn and lil Jim and partly to ensure that New Girl Judy would be included in the ridiculous farm fantasy.

"Sure why not?" Ben said.

"Whatever. You guys have fun on your farm, I'd still rather be able to order pizza." lil Jim said sulkily but without confrontation.

"Speaking of. We need to make a beer run." Shawn said, changing the subject with his slightly confusing segue.

"Speaking of what?" Ben asked.

"Pizza and beer and the rapid availability of both within the city limits. I naturally associate beer with pizza and thusly made the cognitive leap." Shawn said trying to sound more intelligent than he actually was.

"You guys have fun with all that, I think I'm going home." Fat Jenny said to all who cared to listen as she started to stand.

"Really? Come on. Stay." Shawn said. He wanted her to stay so she would pack another bowl but tried to mask this desire by pretending to desire her company. He also noticed New Girl Judy was getting up to go with her.

"No. I've gotta get up early." she said standing and straightening the fold of her colorful dress. "Some of us have class occasionally."

"I have *class* all the time." Shawn replied though no one acknowledged the joke. New Girl Judy smiled at him as he walked them to the door.

"Okay. See ya." the others called out from Ben and Shawn's mutual living room as New Girl Judy and Fat Jenny walked into the hallway while Shawn held the door acting more gentlemanly than necessary or usual.

"Yeah, later days." Fat Jenny called to the crowd left in Ben's living room.

"Days later." Shawn said back to her his head still hanging out the door of his new apartment as he watched New Girl Judy's fishnet shuffle down the hall.

-

Ben woke up to the drone of a bus dragging its sorry load down Harrison Street towards Main. It was off in the distance but with the windows wide open for the small amount of air they brought in the sounds of the city couldn't help but wake him too early. Rina lay next to him on his mattress tangled in sheets soaked with his sweat. He felt disoriented and distracted. He drank too much last night, but then again so did everyone else. The overpainted white door to his bedroom was half open and revealed the living room couch still askew from last night's fun and games.

 Underneath the monotone roar of the bus now disappearing down Harrison, Ben could hear the clanking clanging of construction equipment somewhere in the undetermined distance. He couldn't tell what they were doing from the sound but guessed it was some sort of renovation down the street. Ben's entire street and several blocks beyond that were cheap rentals for college students too poor and uninformed to complain about leaking faucets and water damaged ceilings. Most people on his block never lived there for more than a year or two. Ben had lived here for four years, with no end in sight. Still things would be cheaper now that Shawn was moving in. He would save money on rent. Shawn would live in the living room, such as it was. And Ben would try and spend most nights at Rina's place several blocks away in a much nicer building. Shawn snored on the couch in the other room. Berto had stayed and crashed on the floor along with his ever-present partner lil Jim. Those two were always together. Berto running around like some deep thinking art-fag and lil Jim dogging his every idiotic move. Rina was still asleep and Ben decided not to get up. He'd wake up later and deal with the aftermath of beer cans and empty pizza boxes that Shawn had brought in his wake. For now, he just wanted peace and quiet, as hard as that was to get with the early morning renovations down the street. Ben closed his eyes and tried to force the sounds out of his head as he attempted drift away again.

-

Outline of a dream:

We are asleep you and I. It's a beautiful day outside. The sun is shining the grass is bright green and the lawns are all trimmed beautifully but you and I are asleep on the grass on the front lawn. We are naked. The two of us lie there naked on someone's front lawn with the sun shining on us. It feels so good even though I'm a little embarrassed because everyone can see. I try to wake you up but you don't want to get up so I just lie there with my face nuzzled into the back of your neck. Sleeping. Suddenly there a more people around. Hundreds of people. Waiting. All of them waiting but barely even paying attention to us. They are all parents. Parents who are waiting for their children to get home from school. The buses are just starting to arrive. I wake you up and tell you to get dressed before the children see us. I don't want the children to see us. The dream ends.

10

The houses all along Floyd Avenue stood shoulder to shoulder against the wind. Their large gaping eye windows and long choral mouth doors howled silently at the life streaming in and out of them. Brown and orange leaves blew down the street amidst bits of unidentifiable garbage and cigarette butts. Shawn pulled his black heavily worn and faded leather tighter around him. He hadn't thought to dress in layers and had just run out of the house in a t-shirt and his jacket. He regretted it now. He hadn't the sense for survival that Ben seemed to have. Shawn didn't feel he needed it. He needed it now. He had come back to Floyd to check his mail. He hadn't left any forwarding address and his mother was still sending him the occasional card and quick little note at his old address.

He'd been living at Ben's place for a couple of months now and the fall weather was starting to kick in. It came and went, teasing and taunting everyone. Defying them to dress for the cold; it would run and hide away for the better part of the week out in the foothills of the Blue Ridge to their west only to return the moment Shawn got used to the warm weather again. Every year it was the same. The nights in October would get bitterly cold; then for a week or two in November everyone would wear shorts and talk about the impending destruction of global warming. Whether it was coming or not, Shawn didn't care. He just wanted it to be cold…or warm…or at least one thing at a time. It was the shifts back and forth that drove him crazy and caught him off his guard with bitter fall winds winding their way to the inside of his jacket to freeze him through his threadbare white t-shirt.

It wasn't a long walk from Grace to Floyd but Shawn felt every step in the wind. He shivered out the last of the cold as he stepped inside his old apartment building and closed the heavy door that never quite closed directly behind him. The usual pile of mail greeted him as always. He wondered if it was the tenants that made this mess or if the mailman was just lazy. Perhaps the mailman just opened the door a crack and threw the mail inside rather than place it neatly in little piles. That would explain how it scattered haphazardly about the floor. Or maybe it was the tenants after all. Shawn shifted through the pile roughly, scattering some of it onto the floor himself. He scanned the addressees looking for his name. He didn't find it.

It had been a couple of months now since he moved out. He probably wouldn't come back. It was more than likely that Mom wouldn't be sending any more money. She had sent a few hundred dollars to him. Cash. She shouldn't send cash in the mail but she did anyway, and Shawn had begun to look forward to her bi-weekly installments. He had known it couldn't last when it started, but it had kept him going nonetheless. He would have to learn to live on what he had left, and come up with something to do now.

-

New Girl Judy liked Shawn. He was fun. And cool. Not quite in shape but not fat or anything. She didn't like wussy guys. Guys who were all soo sensitive and nice to you all the time. What's the point? She could have any nice guy she wanted. But Shawn. There was just something about him. He scared her a little bit. He was dangerous. He seemed to know things. Lots of things. He was older of course, and he knew everything about the city. He knew little nooks and hideaway places in the back alleys that they would go to on their long walks at night. He showed her special places. It was kind of romantic in a way. At night when everything was quiet and they were out wandering stoned or drunk through the alleys between the streets, he would show her places like the concrete park between Grove and Park Ave. Or the little brick garden in between Franklin and Grace. He had once lifted her over a puddle in the middle of the alley just past behind the bar at Lombardy. New Girl Judy thought it was the most romantic thing anyone had ever done for her. There was just something about him. And he had so many friends. Of course she already knew Fat Jenny. New Girl Judy and Rina got along well and New Girl Judy was smart enough not to ask Rina anything about Shawn. She could tell there was some history there but felt like it was best just to let it go. Berto was cute in a goofy way but lil Jim stared at her too much. Way too much.

 Shawn was so smart and funny. His accent turned her on even though it seemed not quite real to her. She just loved to hear him talk. She just loved to be around him, in his presence. He made her feel special. Chosen somehow. Worthy. That's why she had melted at his romantic gestures. He was so cool. So together and confident, and he wanted her. How could she have denied him?

-

"Decadence man, it's all about decadence." Shawn tilted his head back, leaning it against the brick of the low rectangular shaped alcove on the train track bridge. The bridge sat a good two hundred feet above the rocky river below but in the dark it felt like five thousand. The alcoves were interspersed along it on either side at about fifty feet apart. In the dark chilly fall air Shawn could just barely make out the next one down the tracks on the opposite side. He didn't know where Berto and Fat Jenny had gotten off to. He didn't know where lil Jim was at all. Shawn would even be inclined to leave him here if he didn't show up at the cars when Shawn wanted to leave; not that he wanted to be deliberately mean he just didn't like being inconvenienced by someone he didn't like.

"You're full of shit." Ben replied dismissively keeping his back firmly against the wall of the brick and his ass planted to the concrete below him. The train would be coming soon and Shawn was just jabbering away like nothing was going on. Jabbering away about nothing as usual.

"Am not." Shawn replied knowing full well that he was always full of shit and Ben knew it.

"You know I'm right." Shawn smiled a derisive smile that no one could see or appreciate. It was two in the morning.

"I think you're both full of shit." Rina said loudly trying to make her voice carry above Shawn and Ben.

"At least I can admit I'm full of shit." Ben said and scooted a little further back into his seat.

"Neither of us is full of shit. But that's your problem. You think you are." Shawn said. "That's why you'll never find it."

"Find what?" Ben asked knowing full well what Shawn was referring to and hoping he would just let it go even though a part of him knew Shawn never could. Shawn was always doing this; waxing philosophical about life or his existence. Getting high and blathering on; that's was all he'd been doing for awhile.

"The meaning of life." Shawn said without a hint of sarcasm in his voice. He believed his own bullshit; or at least made it appear as if he did.

"What the fuck?" Rina asked. Ben looked over at her and could just make out her face which was staring at Shawn like he was a moron. She hadn't dated him long enough for him to start doing this to her so she wasn't used to it. Every time Shawn got high, really high, he started to talk like this. Ben used to like it. It was kind of entertaining at first. But lately Shawn had started to lose his grip a little. He was talking like this more and more. Talking like he knew some great secret thing about life. Some secret thing that Ben hadn't figured out. Ben didn't really care for it.

"The meaning of life. That's what we are all here for isn't it?" Shawn raised his arms in a mockery of a grand gesture that roughly approximated a Jesus-like lifting of his arms towards heaven. Ben wasn't sure if Shawn believed in heaven. But then again, Ben wasn't sure if he believed in heaven either.

"I thought we were here to watch a train." Ben said as Shawn stood up and craned his neck backwards to look at the stars.

"That too. But that's all part of it." Shawn waved his arms up and down and smiled. His facial expressions were more visible outside of the alcove amidst the faint moonlight. "That's all part of it." He said.

"What are you talking about?" Rina said through a hazy gaze and slurred speech that revealed her own intoxicated state.

"The usual," Ben said "decadence, the meaning of existence. You know stoner talk." He shrugged his shoulders and looked back at Shawn who just stared silently at the stars. Ben thought he might end up falling backwards onto the tracks. He imagined what it might be like if Shawn died. The confusion. The torn up body. What would they do?

"What about decadence and the meaning of life?" Rina liked being in the conversation even if she didn't have much to say and only asked questions.

"Decadence is my whole problem." Ben said as they watched Shawn dance on the tracks waiting for the train.

"It is?" Rina rested her head on Ben's shoulder. She wanted to go home. It was late, but they had been waiting for the train for so long now that she couldn't ask to leave. She wasn't afraid anyway. Just tired.

"No." Ben said because he didn't believe Shawn was right, but it confused Rina.

"Huh?" Rina asked.

"You allow your own decadence to be the hindrance to your enlightenment." Shawn contradicted Ben and interrupted. "What you need to do is let it be the gateway. You need to learn from it."

He squatted down in front of where Ben and Rina were sitting, facing the alcove.

"How do you learn from it? And what do you learn from it?" Rina asked Shawn smiling, giggling at his pompousness. She was simultaneously repulsed by him and attracted to his cocky belief in himself. Whatever bullshit he was spreading; he at least did a good job.

"It's hard to say," Shawn said looking at Rina "but it does teach me something about the nature of my own existence. You see. The problem you have is that you think you need to achieve some pure state of being in order to be happy or enlightened or closer to God, whatever." Shawn was looking at Ben. "But you don't."

"We don't?" Rina answered back.

"When have I ever given you the impression that I believe in God at all?" Ben asked Shawn.

"You do. We all do, in our own way; but most of us think we have to appease him or be like him in order to curry his favor. But we don't. None of us do. We are all perfect beings, just as we are. "Shawn smiled his winning smile and sat down again next to Ben and Rina in the alcove of the train bridge.

"So you're perfect and all the rest of us should be like you and live a life of depravity. Decadence? You're saying that decadence is the key to enlightenment and saving our souls?" Rina asked across Ben who sat in the middle tired of this conversation. He didn't need to be told what the meaning of life was. Not by anybody. He had enough life to know there wasn't any meaning to it. You just do the best you can with what you have. He stared at the sky and absorbed the blurry mess of clouds and stars.

"No." Shawn said loudly and crossly in a way that was only possible with an accent. His words and tone said 'I'm mad' but his accent hinted 'not really'. "It's not that decadence is the key. Or even that we need to save our souls. What we need to realize is that we don't need to save ourselves."

"No offense, but you are not exactly saved or enlightened by any stretch of the imagination." Rina said unflustered and intrigued by Shawn's sense of self righteousness.

"That's what *I'm* saying." Shawn said.

"So decadence is the path? But you are not enlightened?" Rina asked.

"Decadence is my path. Not necessarily everyone's. But it works for me."

"So does it bring you closer to God?"

"Well…I am God. In a manner of speaking." Shawn stammered a bit as he said this out loud almost as if he hadn't meant to.

"Um what?" Rina laughed out loud at him. "Maybe I should tell the others. Don't you think everyone would want to know about this?"

"Not like that." Shawn said dismissively. "I am a part of God, just like you are. Just like we all are. If God is perfect, and we are all a part of him. How can anything we do be wrong?" he waved his hands around in tiny circles illustrating his point in the dark. "Isn't it all just a part of his plan? I'm supposed to be a fuck up. I am supposed to live in decadence and depravity. It must be teaching me something." Shawn concluded rather satisfied with himself.

"So you say. I still like beauty." Ben replied addressing Shawn's earlier point about his personal hang-ups.

"Interesting, you still refer to God as a *him*." Rina said.

"It's a hang-up." Shawn said shrugging. "Everything is beautiful, in its own way. You just need to learn how to see it. Take for instance these train tracks and all the industrial fallout around us. You could look at it and see it as ugly. Or you could see a certain kind of rough beauty in all of it. The rust the orange and dirty decay of it all."

"But you're just arguing in extremes. It's easy to see it that way. To see things as beautiful when they're an extreme state, like the perfect balance of nature or the empty wasteland of an abandoned industrial lot. It's a lot harder to find it somewhere in between. It's a lot harder to find beauty in that big empty gray middle." Rina said stealing glances down the tracks and waiting for the train.

"We see what we see." Shawn said in answer to her insight, incapable of carrying his argument about the nature of life any further. He hadn't considered it like that before. He was just looking at the extremes. He was living the extremes. He had always viewed his life as a choice. He could be the 'good boy' his parents wanted him to be. The 'good boy' he felt he should be. Or he could be the 'bad boy' that he was now. The 'bad boy' that he wanted to be. He did everything that way. He did everything he could to cultivate that image. Didn't everyone? He had always seen his options as one or the other. He could be either or.

"But we live there in the middle of that; in between good and bad in big cloud of mediocrity. That's where all of us are." Rina said continuing her point. "I think that's where it's hardest to find meaning. But that's where we have to. If we don't find it here we won't find it at all."

"You find it where you want, and I find it where I want." Shawn said too stoned and to continue talking as his mind reeled with his new realization. Rina let it drop. Ben waited for the train.

-

Outline of a dream:

I am walking down the street. I don't know what street. But I am coming to the end of it. At the crosswalk there is a girl standing. She is wearing a short skirt that is made out of denim and is torn and frayed along the bottom seam. She has on dark stockings and a little jean jacket that is more for fashions sake than any ability it has to provide warmth or protection from the elements. She is very attractive in her outfit and her spiky hair with its pink tinting on the tips. She is a little punk rocker. Cute. She has an attitude and she turns around to face me and shows me her tits. She smiles conspiratorially at me but doesn't say anything. I wrap my arm around her waist and draw her body to me. I kiss her hard and she opens her mouth. We keep kissing for a while and I grab her tits and ass as I pull up her skirt. I keep kissing her but her face begins to morph and change. She is smiling at me but she is not the same person. She looks like a boy I know. I know him but not well. We went to school together. He smiles that cocky smile he always smiled at school whenever he did something bad in class. We fall to the ground and keep making out then he pushes me away and gets up to walk away. The dream ends.

-

"Train!" Shawn yelled down the tracks at Berto and lil Jim who were standing about ten yards away from the alcove they had chosen with Fat Jenny. Their alcove sat roughly fifty yards from Ben, Rina, and Shawn's. The gravel under Berto's feet crunched and crackled as he walked as fast as he dared to despite his fear of the impending train. The whistle blew in the distance and he quickened his pace. The train bridge had no guard rails and despite the fact that it was at least thirty feet wide Berto felt the constant threat of falling. Lil Jim ran behind him oblivious to the danger that creeped up Berto's spine like a chill wind.

Fat Jenny was already safely in the alcove and Berto sat next to her as Jim dawdled in behind him and rested his butt on the cold concrete. "How long do we have?" Berto asked with a tremble in his voice that Fat Jenny decided to ignore for his sake and lil Jim was too stoned to notice.

"Less than two minutes, I think." she said as she blew out a puff of acrid smoke laced with the faintest hint of sweetness that teased at Berto's nostrils while they waited.

The concrete was cold and froze Berto's behind through his black jeans. He was wearing layers but not on his legs. He moved closer to Fat Jenny and she moved closer to him. Lil Jim in turn moved closer to Berto making him feel cramped. He briefly imagined the train somehow vibrating the concrete alcove so much that it detached from the bridge. He thought of himself and Fat Jenny and lil Jim falling down to the rocks and the cold water of the river below them amidst a cascading spread of concrete bits and pieces. It was all a very theatrical scene. Seeing himself falling wedged in-between Lil Jim and Fat Jenny made him feel safer. He imagined that being in-between them; would somehow save him. He imagined that they would somehow absorb all the shock and terrifying blows of the fall and he would walk out unscathed. It made him feel better about the oncoming train.

"thooooo-thoooooo" the train whistled again and Berto could tell it was much closer.

Lil Jim suddenly leaned forward, sticking his head out of the alcove they were all perched in. Berto nearly screamed but managed to keep his discomfort to himself. "I can see it!" lil Jim cried above the roar of the oncoming train that was starting to drown out all the other sounds of the otherwise quiet night that had reigned previously.

Berto reached forward and grabbed the top of lil Jim's jeans. Berto jerked him back hard and lil Jim landed with a huff that scared Berto into thinking he might knocked the wind out of the little guy. It pissed lil Jim off but he smiled instead of saying anything to Berto about it. Instead, he said "Train's coming." Lil Jim said it with a degree of malice that he knew Berto couldn't hear as the train bore down on them.

Fat Jenny grabbed onto Berto's arm as the train sped past them. Its immensity scared the hell out Berto more than he would later admit to anyone. They were all of them only a few feet away from the lumbering velocity that could tear their bodies to pieces if they dared get in its way. The thought of a train derailing and utterly destroying his body fascinated lil Jim to no end and he shouted something to this effect in Berto's left ear as they watched the train; though Berto only vaguely understood his meaning as he spoke. The lights of the train whirred past in streaks and flashes that were broken up by occasional glimpses of the other side of the tracks and the night beyond facilitated by the gaps between the cars. Berto felt immediately uncomfortable with the fact that train cars were wider than the wheels and machining that rode on their tracks and wondered with a suicidal awe at why they didn't just tip off of the seemingly flimsy steel rails. Knowing nothing about physics he could do nothing but fantasize about his own immanent death. Fat Jenny whispered something hot in his right ear and then licked it. The night had been cold up until now. She squeezed his inner thigh when she knew lil Jim wasn't looking. What had she said?

As soon as it had come it was gone and speeding off past the bridge and into the bowels of the night air that was fast returning to its previous serenity.

"That was awesome!" lil Jim said with a huge smile on his face.

"Woo-hoo!" they heard Shawn scream into the dark night from further down the tracks. It had been his idea to come here. He usually wouldn't leave his apartment stoned; but on occasion he would get a great idea. Whenever he had ideas for things, they got done. If they had a leader it was Shawn. And Ben, for better or worse, was his second in command. Ben seconded everything

Shawn wanted. Not because Ben necessarily liked to do these things; he just liked to be a part of things. And that's what Shawn did for him.

11

Rina left with a whimper. Somewhere in the few weeks between the train tracks and the winter break from school she had just wandered away and stopped coming to see Ben. At first Ben blamed Shawn, thinking she was finally fed up with his presence in Ben's apartment, but he knew no one was really to blame. She was beautiful and young and he had ceased to amuse her. It was nothing personal. Nothing personal at all.

Supposedly she still saw Fat Jenny and even Berto and lil Jim occasionally but she was avoiding Ben, for now. He knew the routine of course. Rina would keep her distance for a few weeks, maybe a month or more, then she would come back; quite possibly with a new boyfriend to drift in and out of their circle of friends. Ben would probably even like the guy. He would have no hard feelings as they say. He had done this before. He had the good fortune to have at least had a girlfriend or two in the past; though he kept the exact number to himself because it couldn't compare to Shawn's uncountable conquests. Rina had been special though.

She had come into both their lives with such a clamor and wonder. Doe-eyes looking for sin behind thin dark rimmed glasses. She was a petite, black-haired beauty that wanted them both alternately and loved to stay up late listening to their idiotic ramblings and stories. And she loved sex. Shawn, of course, was used to that kind of attention from girls; but Ben, rarely. Though it was not from lack of trying. He just wasn't as charismatic as Shawn. And his bad eye and welfare driven lifestyle didn't bode well for him in his attempts to attract the opposite sex. Rina had seemed to not care about any of it. She liked his life. She liked the way he lived, where he lived. The things he was usually ashamed to have to admit to, she seemed to accept without judgment. She was even more or less turned on by it.

But deep down Ben knew what all that had really meant. She was slumming, and he was the slum. For some unknowable reason Rina had decided to crawl into the gutter for awhile and when she discovered that Shawn wasn't far enough in, she turned to Ben. Ben was the gutter. He was the bottom. Hopeless, crippled and high, but well built. Ben had a strong body and that at least had appealed to Rina. Even if, as he suspected, his grimaced face and malfunctioning eye had repulsed her. That eye, which he had tried in vain during the tenure of their relationship to always hide from her, had marked and dominated his existence for as long as he could remember. It had kept him from everything he had ever dreamed of. It had kept him even from dreaming. Now it had cost him Rina.

He almost wanted to say he loved her but the thought was too laughable for him to entertain. He didn't dare feel love for her. He couldn't afford it. He knew he couldn't afford it when they had started dating and he knew it now even more acutely as he sat in his bedroom listening to the constant hiss of the ancient radiator in the corner of his bedroom.

The landlord had finally turned on the heat now that it was mid-December and winter was officially declared. The leaking radiators never stopped their tireless, low level hissing now. If Ben had other things going on he hardly heard the three radiators in his one-bedroom but not today. Today the radiator did nothing to drown out the sounds of New Girl Judy and Shawn in the other room; fucking behind Shawn's flannel sheets in the early morning thinking Ben was still asleep. He wished he was. He wished they would stop so he could go to the kitchen and get something to eat from the meager leftovers in the fridge. He wished a lot of things but none of them were about to come true any time soon.

\-

The fact that New Girl Judy didn't mind sleeping in the living room was a great boon to Shawn. He had marked off his little arena with a set of heavy flannel sheets stapled to the ceiling. Their paisley pattern reminded Shawn in some vague way of a hippie apartment he had seen in an episode of Dragnet in re-runs. He snickered at the look of it when he had done it and thought himself at the pinnacle of bohemian decadence until that is he had invited New Girl Judy into his boudoir. The sight of her strutting around his little enclave of scattered sheets, paisley and incense was more of a turn on than he could imagine. Her puffy soft nipple sat atop breasts that nearly stood at attention outside of their bra. They were full and round and complimented her chubby thighs well. She was a system of curvaceous delight and her shadow on the wall did almost as much for him as the mirror he and Ben had jerry-rigged to the ceiling. The sight of her riding on top of him did a lot to enhance his pleasure with her. Each hard thrust upward as they fucked sent her tits bouncing in a cascade that he could enjoy in double vision.

As she ground herself to her second orgasm of the morning on top of him New Girl Judy started to think about Ben in the other room. She was getting louder and bolder the more time she spent with Shawn. He wasn't exactly a divine physical specimen but he was fun to be with. She worried that she was going to wake Ben up. Though she knew that he knew she and Shawn were sleeping together it still violated a particular bit of social propriety for her to know that he could hear her having sex. The paisley sheet walls of Shawn's enclave were beyond thin. They were sheets. Even flannel couldn't muffle the sounds of her moaning. Not that Shawn wanted her to keep quiet. He liked Ben to know what a good lover he was. He told her so. Shawn wanted everyone to know. New Girl Judy believed he would be willing to have sex in front of everyone just to prove it. She didn't know the limits to his kinky side and that both scared and excited her.

As the spasms in her body subsided she slumped on top of Shawn's bare and mostly hairless blond chest, sweaty and starting to feel the chill of the December air creeping in from gaps in the rickety window panes of the second floor apartment. Shawn rolled her over onto her back to finish himself off and she watched his buttocks jiggle with each thrust in the mirror above their heads as she lay there. She had breakfast on her mind now that she was awake and satiated. Shawn soon would too.

-

Outline of a dream:

I am in the park. Or walking into the park. Down by the river. But everything is starting to flood. You are nowhere to be found and I don't know where I last saw you. For some reason I have two cameras. One is yours and one is mine. I am with several different guys who all seem to know each other and they all know me. They talk to me as if we have been friends for years and yet I don't recognize any of them. They laugh and joke with me but I detect a secret hint of malice in their words and jibes.

I keep losing my grip on the cameras as I try to hold them both in one hand. It is raining really hard and everybody has on raincoats. All the coats are different colors. We keep walking down a path and I can see water running through the trees. It's the river. I see that it's rising. I am scared for you. Where are you?

A new guy shows up and greets us. The others know him. He is covered in mud all over his body. Only his face is clear. He was in the river. The river is all muddy. Everybody laughs. He laughs. I don't get the joke. They don't care about the flood. I think we might all die. We have to keep moving I say the water is rising. I can see it on the path we are on. It's forming into big deep puddles and starting to flow together. I drop the cameras. They were too slippery.

Everybody laughs. They say the world is going to end. Why do cameras matter? I wonder where you are as I clean off the cameras and hope that they aren't too wet. I decide to give up. They are all laughing at me. The dream ends.

-

Lil Jim looked at Ben sympathetically from the couch in Fat Jenny's apartment. They were in a rough circle strewn across Fat Jenny's eclectic furniture. He, Berto, Jack, and Denny were sharing a bowl lil Jim had just packed.

"Dude what the fuck is up with this thing?" Jack asked as rudely as possible.

"It's the wonky bowl!" Berto said laughing to himself when no one joined him. Jack looked at the brass contraption derisively and handed it over to Denny whose eyes had glazed over.

"I'm sorry about Rina." Lil Jim said to Ben who didn't seem to be looking at him.

"Thanks but, it's not a big deal. Had to end sometime." Ben said with a shrug. He wondered what was keeping Shawn and Fat Jenny. They had left over an hour ago to get Chinese food from the place on Grace Street a meager four blocks from Ben's apartment. He had offered to go with them but for some reason they both said no. Berto had demanded to not, and lil Jim didn't get a vote. Everybody knew Jack wasn't going to do anything but at least he had brought the weed. Ben didn't like Jack but he tolerated him because Shawn did.

"Whatever man." Jack said to no one who was listening even though Ben knew he was talking to him. "Who cares about that stupid bitch? If it was me I'd just go out and find some other bitch and fuck her tonight!" Jack smiled at himself and the level of nasty that he could affect. Berto snickered and coughed hard as the smoke burned the inside of his sinuses. Ben was fairly certain that Jack would do no such thing if a girl as fine as Rina had shared the better part of four months in his bed. Ben was fairly sure that no girl had ever shared Jack's immense bulk for more than a night, and if that, reluctantly. It was a defense. It all was. Berto's snickering, Jack's callousness, even Denny's stoner façade with his glazed over eyes and silent drooping gaze, even Ben' own silent dismissing shrug. They could all be hurt they just pretended not to be.

Ben chose to ignore Jack's high pitched whinny of a laugh at his expense. He had little choice. Instead he just shrugged and let his gaze drift as the smoked curled out of his mouth.

"Whatever." He said.

Ben wasn't the only guy who had lost a girlfriend lately anyway. Shawn was in the same boat as he was. New Girl Judy had just disappeared. Not even Fat Jenny, who acted as the hub of the gossip wheel could tell Shawn what had happened to her. She seemed to have stopped talking to everyone almost overnight. Fat Jenny suspected she had 'pulled a D' as she called it.

Two years ago, back when Fat Jenny was the freshman girl creeping out to Shawn's apartment for an education in sex and drugs and the decadent lifestyle Shawn preached, she had been dragging around a cute little girl by the name of D. D not knowing anyone and being Fat Jenny's roommate followed nervously but eagerly behind to engage in every depraved experiment that Shawn and Fat Jenny dared to explore. Less than two weeks after D first tried LSD with Fat Jenny and Shawn on a biting February night; D had packed all of her belongings and headed home halfway through her second semester at school. D had a bad trip. A scary trip. Some people do. Shawn and Fat Jenny hadn't done anything peculiar or scary, but D was one of those troublingly vulnerable people for whom psychotropic substances are extremely unsettling. D eventually came back to town but never returned to school. She had apparently spent the better part of two months sleeping on the couch in front of the television. Afraid to move, her parents had no idea what to do with her, and they almost committed her. To Shawn, it was one of the silliest things he had ever heard. He had cracked the shell around D's little mind and she nearly went over the edge. Just like that OJ guy, Shawn thought. Goddamn orange juice for a brain.

Ben wondered if New Girl Judy would be back. He couldn't remember her doing any heavy drugs since she'd been around but how was he to know for certain? Shawn had a way of getting people in over their heads. He lived that way; over his head. Out there drowning in an urban sea of decadence that he willingly called forth. But Ben suspected that Shawn had a life raft, even if he was on the outs with momanddad, Shawn had an out. A life-boat on the sea just waiting for him. And Ben hoped he at least had a seat in the back.

New Girl Judy might come back. Some do. Some don't. It was a stupid time of life really. For every one of them. Ben looked around at the kids that surrounded him. They leave their parents' house eager for freedom and some twisted dream of independence only to run back to momanddad the minute anything goes awry. What, he wondered, did they think independence was? Ben had never had momanddad. He never had anybody. Except for maybe Shawn.

"Still, I'm sorry man." lil Jim said. "She was hot."

"Yeah." They all agreed.

Jack packed the bowl again and thrust it at Ben without a word. This was his way of commiserating even if he could never actually vocalize sympathy. It wasn't in his nature and Ben knew it. Or rather Ben knew that it wasn't in the nature of the character Jack was playing at the time. The immense NOVA punk with the pencil thin mohawk grin and his predatory smile, rested back on the couch causing the whole thing to groan under him. His clean blue jeans and leather were immaculate in stark contrast to Ben's clothes that he had been wearing for three days. It was getting towards mid-month and he was trying to stretch his dollars. It amazed him that Jack could believe his own bullshit. Or at least give such a good impression of believing his own bullshit. But then that was how things were. Jack needed to believe his own bullshit. It gave him identity. It gave him meaning. It made Ben question himself. Maybe Jack just was this fat fucking asshole and Ben was just making all this up. Ben took his hit off the bowl and passed to Berto to his left without looking at him. He decided not to think about Jack anymore. He didn't like having that fucker in his thoughts and the weed was getting to him. Where were Shawn and Fat Jenny anyway?

-

Knowing that New Girl Judy was out of the picture and that everybody was over at her place while they waited for her and Shawn to get back from the food run, Fat Jenny had kept an ear perked up for any hint of a proposition from Shawn as they went. They had danced the bed dance a few times in the past. Never with any regularity or seriousness and always with a mutual consent towards non-exclusivity that kept them both free and capable of fucking whomever; whenever they chose. Fat Jenny was used to this kind of arrangement, and had learned to steel her heart against any would be suitors as a result. Her arrangement with Berto was much the same. This was, in fact, the arrangement all her recent lovers had opted for. Berto was no different from Shawn, or Ken, or Russell. She was the fat girl and they wanted skinny girls to date. They wanted skinny girls on their arms to show off to an adoring public. She was used to her lovers being embarrassed of her. She told herself it didn't matter. It didn't matter because they still came back. They came back and she could pretend, at least within the confines of their secret embraces, that there was something special between them. And when they left, she could go back to pretending that it didn't matter.

She had toughened up quite a bit since she had been left by her high school boyfriend while professing her undying love to him in the back of her red hatchback. Crying as he told her he was breaking it off.

She hadn't had anyone ever profess his undying love to her, but she was still young enough to believe it would be happening soon. However, that didn't stop her from taking the opportunity to practice her skills when an opportunity arose. And Shawn was definitely an opportunity about to happen.

There had been some need to go to his apartment. Some insignificant, innocent need to go there. To the apartment he shared with Ben. The apartment that was now vacant because Ben was waiting at her apartment. It gave them privacy and time. The unmistakable gleam in Shawn's eye bespoke her unvoiced anticipation. Everything else was just a ruse. They both wanted this. She wasn't after Shawn. He was definitely not after her. He just wanted a roll, as did she.

The real trick was not letting Berto know and Shawn knew that as well as she did. Berto talked a good line about no strings and freedom, but when it came right down to it; he wanted her all for his own. Not because he wanted her but because he didn't want anyone to have what he considered his. Not that he could admit this to himself. It would be an insult to him. It would wound his fragile sense of machismo and leave just enough of a scab for him to pick at and pick at until it was a gushing melodramatic, unnecessary wound. Berto was a boy, pretending to be a man; so he acted like he thought a man should act. And Shawn, though not quite a man, at least knew a few things about discretion. So she and Shawn would keep it quiet. It might only be this one time for them. "Just a little fucking to brighten an otherwise dreary December."
Shawn would say afterwards. Just a little indeed.

-

Outline of a dream:

Everything is white. Office space. Doctor's office? No, dentist office. Aren't dentists doctors? Fuck if I know. Hot dental assistant is walking in front of me. She's wearing one of those really short skirts that buttons all the way up the front. Dental assistants don't really wear those do they? When was the last time I was in the dentist's office? I don't know. But she's dressed like we are in a porn movie. She's too shapely to be here. A body like that doesn't work in the dentist's office. We walk past a room. People are having sex in there. Not people, men. Big men; these guys are huge. Body builder types. I've never seen one in person. Only on TV. Shapely, muscular; they have big wide grins. Ultra-males. They're fucking. Well one is going down on the other. He sits in that weird dentist chair that half reclines but he is leaning forward. Everything else in the room is blurry but this huge guy sucking this other body builder's dick. Everything about them is huge. The hot dental assistant disappears. Everything remains blurry but the bodybuilders. They're clear and bright. The dream ends.

12

Ben eyed Shawn suspiciously as he wandered around their cold living room aimlessly. It had been three days since the winter holiday for the university had begun and neither of them was faring well. After having exhausted Ben's motley supply of ancient VHS tapes on the first day they lacked the motivation to watch them again and the creeping frozen boredom of winter in the city had begun to set in. Since neither of them had anywhere to go and nearly everyone of consequence they knew was now out of town they had both resigned themselves to a couple of weeks meting out the days in their cold apartment. Ben hadn't expected the boredom to come so fast but then again he hadn't counted on Shawn.

Ben could fare quite well on his own and he had always assumed Shawn could as well until recently. Ben survived mainly on minor routines and rituals that no one else was invited to participate in. He made daily trips to stores and frequented the same haunts he did during the regular school year just without any companionship. He had long hours in front of cold windows to keep him occupied as he watched blurry shapes whiz below him on the streets. He had coffee and empty booths to wander through at the Village down the corner as he drank and sulked and tried not to notice the growing similarities between himself and the old men who showed up at the bar at seven in the morning. He had survived the boredom of five (or more?) winters in the city. In short, he lived, quietly and without expectation. Shawn was a different story altogether.

Now that Shawn was here and was without New Girl Judy's companionship, Ben felt a need to entertain him and had in fact been indulging him since he had moved in. With both of them single and the winter break underway their lives had slowed to an imperceptible crawl that was starting to drive Shawn crazy. Shawn flopped onto the dank yellow settee which had once occupied a prominent space in his smoking room. He huffed a little and a small cloud of steam reported on the temperature difference between his lungs and the cold air of their apartment. The radiators hissed uselessly and unnoticed in the far corner of the room. Shawn tucked his hands under either arm and pulled his legs up onto the settee and underneath himself sitting cross-legged. He looked to Ben rather like a vagrant Eskimo in his dirty oversized sweater and heavy cap. It had gotten bitterly cold and Shawn wasn't handling it well.

"I'm bored." Shawn said exasperatedly as if he had been trying to accomplish some Herculean feat for the last two hours and had finally given up.

"Sorry." Ben replied holding a cup of bad coffee. He held his coffee with both hands and had been leaching the warmth from it privately until Shawn started huffing. Shawn's presence made it impossible for Ben to stare emptily off into space.

"Let's do something." Shawn demanded. They had had this same conversation for three mornings in a row and it always ended the same.

"What do you want to do?" Ben asked right on cue. He knew Shawn would have no answer. Shawn wanted something but he had no idea what.

"I dunno." Shawn replied following his script perfectly. Now it was Ben's turn to reply with the only idea he had in the past three days.

"Do you want to go out and get some coffee?" Ben asked knowing full well that they had plenty of coffee sitting in the pot behind them but Shawn needed the stimulus of the Village café.

Shawn needed to move, to be outside. Shawn couldn't stand for sitting still. He needed some version of forward momentum even if that momentum took him nowhere. It was oddly different from how Ben thought of Shawn, what had changed?

"Yes." Shawn replied happily. They would undoubtedly get breakfast there as they had the three mornings previous. At least they were doing something.

-

Outline of a dream:

I am in a class. I think it's a science class? There are frogs and high tables. We are all on uncomfortable stools. I don't know why we are here. I am not in any science class. I feel young, and little. I am little. The teacher is a woman. Not old, but not as young as me. She is arguing with me. Disapproving. I know something, I am insisting on it but she keeps denying it. She won't listen. I don't understand, But I am getting embarrassed in front of the class. I know I'm right. What are we arguing about? The dream ends.

-

"So what do you think?" Shawn asked with a wry mile on his face as he perused over greasy eggs and overfried hash browns at the Village.

"About what?" Ben asked distractedly sipping his coffee. He only had been half listening to Shawn. This little trip to the Village was blowing his budget for the week. Ben was supposed to be eating in this morning and thus saving some of his government money.

"About what I just told you." Shawn said referring to his story about Fat Jenny and their hook-up. "You know you're getting a little spacey these days." Shawn waggled a finger at Ben and then dismissed him as no longer worth admonishing for not paying attention. He turned his gaze outward towards the street.

"Sorry, I just…I don't know. I mean it's not like they're really dating is it?" Ben said thinking about Berto and wondering if he would care about Fat Jenny cheating on him. He had certainly seen Berto try to hook-up with girls besides Fat Jenny. Berto just didn't have any luck, which to Ben's mind wasn't the same as not actually cheating on Fat Jenny.

"Yeah that's what he said before," said Shawn who was somewhat aware of Berto's incomplete attempts at extracurricular activity. "but I get the feeling that if he knew he'd get pissed you know?" Shawn smiled and Ben could tell he felt ridiculously satisfied with himself that he had pulled one over on Berto and fucked Fat Jenny.

"I guess so. Why'd you do it?" Ben asked.

"Just because, I suppose. I don't really know. Probably just because I could." Shawn munched on his eggs and sipped his coffee intermittently. Ben watched him for some signs of remorse. He didn't see anything.

"I guess that's as good a reason as any." Ben responded and let his blurred gaze drift out the window. He moved his fork across his empty plate and wished he had enough money to order a second breakfast. Shawn was a slow eater and this always made Ben twice as hungry.

"Always is." Shawn said through a mouthful of potatoes and onion. He washed the half chewed mass down with the last of his lukewarm coffee and set the mug to his left at the edge of the table where the waitress could see it. It was his private hint for her to hurry up and bring him another refill. Whether or not she would respond was anybody's guess and Ben was certain she'd get the same tip no matter what she did. "What would you have done?" Shawn said finally with a clear and uncorrupted mouth right before he gobbled down the last bit of his toast that had been smothered in butter and strawberry jam.

"Probably the same, though Fat Jenny's never really turned me on much." Ben shrugged and lied a little about Fat Jenny. Actually he would have loved to roll around with her but the opportunity had never come up. He wondered if it would. "Still, I'd like to know what that would be like. What's it like to have sex with such a big girl?"

"Same as any other girl, just bigger." Shawn said. "Actually I really like fat girls, there's just so much ass to grab."

"But is like the pressure still the same?" Ben said with an awkward squint that at once implied something he was struggling to remember and something he had never truly seen.

"What the fuck are you talking about?" Shawn asked back incredulously making Ben feel embarrassed to ask again.

"I mean inside? You know." Ben said trying not to be too obvious as he shoved forward in his seat to mimic a thrusting motion. Shawn was unsure if this gesture was conscious or unconscious and let it slip past without commenting on it.

"Of all the ridiculous questions." Shawn said melodramatically. "Yes it's the same. It's probably just like you'd imagine. It's just sex anyway. I don't know why everybody makes such a bloody big deal about it." He dismissed Ben's curiosity with a twitchy gesture of his head and looked down the central aisle of the Village for his waitress who had yet to come by with the coffee refill he was in desperate need of.

"You make a big deal about it." Ben said unable to articulate his feelings about sex and sexuality fully.

"Yeah, but I love it." Shawn said flippantly as if people either preferred to have sex or to not have it; like it was a choice among dinner options.

"That's true." Ben said with a sarcastic tone that enticed Shawn to query him.

"What's that supposed to mean?" Shawn asked Ben searching his on eye for the meaning hidden there.

"It means, you know, you sleep with everything in sight. I mean even guys dude." Ben mentioned uncomfortably with a glance sideways and into the aisle of the Village though no one was there to see it besides Shawn.

"I haven't slept with a man in a long time." Shawn said without hesitation, still looking up the aisle for the absent waitress.

"But still." Ben said plainly as if this said everything and Shawn would now exactly what he meant by it.

"Still what?" Shawn said turning his attention away from the aisle with the disappeared waitress. He looked at Ben warily.

"You do. I mean, you have. Right?" Ben said asking openly for the first time what he had always known. Shawn slept with men, when he felt like it.

"Yes, I have." Shawn answered honestly; afraid that he might have to find a new place to live if Ben didn't react well to his answer. "Why do you bring it up? Does this matter to you?"

"No. I just want to know what it's like. It seems weird to me, that you can just substitute one for the other." Ben said.

"Just because you can't doesn't mean I can't. I think you should ask yourself why it is that you can't." Shawn said with a dropped voice and pointed finger as the waitress poured Shawn his fourth cup of coffee.

"I just don't is all." Ben said unapologetically.

"But why?" Shawn asked with a gleam in his eye.

"But why what?" Ben asked him back.

"The thing is, one is better than the other but sometimes the alternative will do, you know?"

Shawn said.

"No." Ben said.

"It's like, you want a cheeseburger, right, but you don't have enough money for a cheeseburger so instead you eat ramen noodles, you know." Shawn spread his hands out before Ben as if their emptiness explained everything. As if Ben would understand this kind of poverty. A poverty of sexual pleasure. A lack of accessibility that had therefore necessitated an adaptation.

"I don't know if I would compare ramen noodles to sex with a man." Ben replied with an unrelenting image of cooked noodles festering inside his head. Ben ate a lot of ramen noodles, and now the image was stuck there. Not just the image, but the whole process. Tearing open the package, the boiling water, draining the noodles into a bowl. It was all there now wrapped up inside Shawn's sex life. Thanks, Ben thought. Thanks a lot.

"Yes, but I would, and that is probably why I get laid more than you." Shawn said and sipped his scalding hot coffee. It always bothered him that he could never get coffee at exactly the right temperature. It always came too hot or not hot enough. Though he believed too hot was the better alternative.

"I don't think that's why." Ben retorted, unsure of himself.

"Yes it is, you could be getting laid right now if you wanted to." Shawn smiled.

"What the hell are you talking about?" Ben looked across the table with his question though Shawn's smile didn't' give anything away.

"What indeed?" Shawn asked.

-

Fat Jenny's surprise visit provided Shawn and Ben a welcome respite from each other's company though Ben was happier than Shawn to see her. Ever since their breakfast conversation at the diner Shawn had been eyeing Ben and dropping subtle hints about the two of them hooking up. It made Ben highly uncomfortable but he could hardly call Shawn out on it. Shawn had plausible deniability. If Ben said anything Shawn would just swear up and down he hadn't meant anything by his comment about being lonely and would then turn the accusations back on to Ben which would only result in making Ben more uncomfortable.

 Fat Jenny sat on the floor of their apartment looking like a flophouse madam in a green and purple patchwork dress that looked different from every angle Shawn looked at it. Ben was in the kitchen preparing a spaghetti feast for the three of them while Shawn laid flat on the floor staring at the ceiling. Fat Jenny sat cross-legged in front of a low table sorting seeds and stems out of a bag of shwag she had brought from home. It wasn't exactly big city fair and it tasted every bit the shit-weed Shawn had heard about coming in from the southern counties.

"Well, it tastes like shit-weed but I'll still smoke it" Shawn said as he double-puffed the joint Fat Jenny had rolled for all three of them when she first got in the door. She smiled a devilish grin and snatched it away from him.

"Ben baby" Fat Jenny called out flirting, "don't you want any of this?" A muffled groan of affirmation rolled in from inside the kitchenette of the one bedroom apartment. Ben walked out with a mouth full of garlic bread.

"Thanbmfs." Ben said as he took a drag off the thin joint. It had been rolled extra tight and the weed was nearly ground into a powder. It hit hard and Ben knew that just this drag would get him high enough to gobble up dinner greedily. He didn't care one way or the other about the taste. He couldn't tell the difference among all the various kinds of weed Fat Jenny brought around. He just knew it got him high. This stuff tasted like…garlic bread with marijuana in it? Oh shit, he was high. He handed the joint back to Fat Jenny and went back into the kitchen to watch the pot of spaghetti noodles intensely. Now that he was stoned there was a good chance he would over cook the whole lot. That wasn't going to be good for anybody.

"How's the spaghetti?" Fat Jenny asked as Ben continued to munch on the garlic bread that now tasted like weed.

"It should be done soon." Ben said automatically not really thinking about his answer as he stood there in front of the pot. Did she just wink at him? It was hard to tell from in here with his one good eye. He could just barely see the details of her face sitting at the table in the living room. The noodles were boiling over the sides of the pot; he had stopped paying attention to them. He had just been staring at Fat Jenny. She laughed at him from the living room and went back to sorting her seeds.

-

Dinner was over-cooked but no one noticed or minded. Fat Jenny sat between them now as all three of them stared vacantly at the television not watching anything in particular. Ben idly held the remote control and flipped through the meager four channels endlessly. He didn't notice Shawn kissing Fat Jenny right away. It started as blurry movement in his peripheral vision. Ben ignored it until the vaguely purplish movement intensified and Fat Jenny pushed into him giggling. Ben looked at her squinting as she pushed on his shoulders causing him to slide sideways and onto his back on the couch. He could barely make out Shawn behind Fat Jenny though he seemed to be lifting up her dress. Fat Jenny laid him flat and fell forward just enough to bring her lips into contact with his. He kissed her out of reflex and she kissed back and giggled again. She kissed his neck and chin and he felt her hands go to his belt and undo it. She moaned a little as Shawn entered her from behind and started pumping forward making her rock back and forth a little above Ben.

"Move up a little." Fat Jenny said as she reached into Ben's undone jeans with one hand. She was unsuccessfully trying to free his dick. Ben wiggled upward on the small couch obligingly but still not sure if he wanted to be a part of this little sexual escapade with Fat Jenny and Shawn. Fat Jenny tugged at the edge of his pants twice with the one hand that wasn't supporting her as she bent over on the couch. "Pull these down for me."

Ben understood her meaning and wiggled his jeans and underwear both down just past his ass freeing his dick which was now rock solid at the prospect of getting blown. Ben's crotch disappeared in a mass of curly red hair and as her warm wet mouth slid over the head of his penis he sighed and shuddered involuntarily. God that felt good. He hadn't gotten laid since Rina and he had been missing it. Fat Jenny rocked forward with every gentle thrust Shawn made which created a very specific rhythm for the blow job she was giving to Ben. Ben reached down the top of her dress and cupped both of her huge breasts. He had to dig for the nipples but when he found the hard tips he smiled. Looking up he saw Shawn smiling back at him.

-

Berto crashed through the living room of his friend's house knocking over an end table. Harmless, but embarrassing nonetheless. Lil Jim had passed out alone upstairs nearly an hour ago and Berto was wandering drunk through the remaining stragglers that had yet to leave. The evening had been a bust for him and lil Jim. Neither one of them had successfully plied their cool older college man shtick well enough to get any action from the high school girls that had come to the party. It wasn't for lack of trying, it was just bad technique. Berto stood in the nearly abandoned living room in his long black coat and smiled at two girls sitting on a couch. In the dim living room of the suburban dream home that belonged to his friend's parents Berto looked as drunk as he was and they were not impressed. Berto couldn't find his friend; so he could only imagine that his friend's efforts at procuring female companionship for the night had been successful. All in all, it had been a fun party; what he could remember of it anyway. The girls on the couch watched him as he swayed back and forth unsteadily. They quickly gathered up their jackets and purses and left, cigarette smoke trailing behind them.

Berto watched their asses as they walked away with a leering grin and then wandered head first for the couch. Lil Jim was unconscious upstairs somewhere and Berto was pretty sure that this was where he was ending the evening. The bad wine was starting to make the room twitch in his vision. The sensation was fascinating when it wasn't nauseating and Berto stared at the ceiling to get the full effect. The light blinded him but he didn't feel capable of getting up to turn it off. He pulled a pillow over his eyes to block out the light and it smelled soothingly of an older woman's perfume. It reminded him of his grandmother or his great aunt. It was their kind of scent. The scent of must and aged flowers, hard candies, and tiny soaps that no one, not even guests, are allowed to use.

The room still spun and twitched with a jerking sensation that pulled his vision back and forth even with his eyes closed and in the darkness afforded by the pillow over his face. Berto wished he had spent more time with lil Jim tonight. If he had known they were both going to end up dateless he wouldn't have tried so hard to get laid. He really wanted to fuck a skinny girl. Just to try something different from Fat Jenny. Poor lil Jim, Berto wasn't sure if he had ever been laid. Berto started to snore with the pillow still perched atop his face.

-

Outline of a dream:

Faces. A ton of faces everywhere and talking. Everybody's smiling, not really at me though. I wander from person to person. All I see are their mouths laughing. Not laughing at me just open.

I see teeth everywhere. Big smiling white teeth. Then a girl. Do I know her? I don't think so. God but she is beautiful. She is thin, blond, short hair. Wearing black jeans and a tight black shirt that doesn't cover her belly entirely. It reminds me of an outfit Rina used to wear. Just enough skin showing to make everybody look. She's beautiful. It try to speak to her but the people get in the way. She recedes into the crowd. I have to follow. Someone asks me something and I turn to look at him. I t doesn't make any sense he says words but I don't understand. They are real words but he doesn't put them together right. He's wearing a loud Hawaiian shirt. It's blue with white flowers. I don't see his eyes they are blurry. He has short hair and a tan. He's muscular under the shirt. I try to turn away but he won't let me go. He just keeps talking. Where did she go? I have to find her. I push through the crowd again but she's gone. I missed my chance. She's gone again. The dream ends.

-

"Hey sleepy." Fat Jenny whispered into his ear as Ben woke up sticky and naked in Shawn's makeshift bedroom of flannel curtains. "I've got to go, but tell Shawn thanks for me when you see him." Fat Jenny stood up fully dressed with her big sack purse hooked under her arm. It was bright and colorful in a way completely opposite that of her dress but she managed to not clash despite herself. She had pulled on a pair of purple tights for the cold weather outside and began rummaging in her purse. Hardly any light drifted through the flannel sheet walls Shawn had erected months ago but Ben could still tell it was daytime.
"Where is Shawn?" Ben asked her confusedly. Bits and pieces of last night were coming back to him in waves of embarrassing realization. It was too late to take any of it back but the fallout was just beginning. He needed to know where Shawn was. A bus roared loudly down Harrison Street. Fat Jenny stood still looking in her purse.

"I don't know where he is. He was gone when I woke up and he's not in your room, I looked. I had hoped we were gonna get another go round but..." she let her voice trail off and her smile do all the talking as she found a rainbow colored stocking cap in her purse and put it on her head. "Maybe when school gets back in session, okay? But I have to go. I'll see you." She waived and parted the flannel sheets in the middle of the living room.

Ben pulled a hand out from under the sheets and returned the wave. "Later days." he said.

"Days later, baby. Days later." Fat Jenny called back as she left, seeing herself out of his apartment.

Ben heard the door click shut and realized he was completely alone in the apartment. Where the fuck was Shawn? Last night played through his head in flashes like a preview for a porn movie. Well, that was that. A three-way with Fat Jenny and Shawn was sure to get around to everybody eventually. Ben lay back down in bed and sighed. At least it had been fun. But now? What was he going to say to Shawn?

13

Things had been quiet for a few days between them. Shawn acted as if nothing spectacular had happened when Fat Jenny had come by to visit with her shit weed and suggestive comments so Ben played along not wanting to rock the boat of their insular world. But then it happened again. Only without Fat Jenny.

Ben was in the shower the first time, when Shawn came in, and stone sober asked if he could join him. Standing on the other side of the curtain Ben questioned whether or not any of this had been a good idea. Letting Shawn move in had been the first mistake. No. Being friends with Shawn had been the first mistake. Was it a mistake? He felt vulnerable, and lost. Standing in the hot stream of water that provided a brief respite from the floating chill in the rest of the apartment he didn't quite know what to do. Getting involved with Shawn could be disastrous. Fuck, it was almost guaranteed to be disastrous. But what could he do? What he wanted to he supposed. He was lonely. Shawn was here. It didn't mean anything anyway. It would just be sex. And just for fun. It wouldn't make him gay. Not that he was really worried about that anyway. What would that even mean: 'Make him gay?' What the fuck did he have to lose even if he was? Would they have ground rules? Would they be in a relationship? Would they still fuck girls? There were too many questions for Ben as he stood there in the shower blurry eyed and wanting some companionship so badly he was even willing to accept Shawn's groping hands for some release. In the moments Ben stood there debating his future or non-future with Shawn; Shawn stepped in the shower and made Ben's decision for him. That was the first time. Four days after Christmas.

 The next time it went easier, no long internal debates, no interior monologues, just release. Ben got used to the differences, and the two of them spent the rest of the winter break alone together.

-

Outline of a dream:

I'm sitting at a table. I'm in the Village. It is night-time outside and it's crowded in here. It must be Saturday. I guess it's late. The table feels greasy under my hands and I keep smearing water stains by accident and getting my hands wet. There are people sitting with me or I'm sitting with them. I'm on the outside seat next to the aisle. The walk. The aisle between the booths that everyone walks down at least once a week. Mostly on Saturdays. People walk the walk to see who's here. Everyone comes here. I look around the table, everything's blurry and all I see are smiles. Stupid smiles loaded with beer and french fries. I don't recognize any of them but I know them all the same. How do I know them? They know me, or seem to, they laugh at me, and they smile.

 I get up and walk out the back to leave. It's hard to move. I feel like I'm walking through soup. I try to hurry, but I only slow down more. There's smoke everywhere and people continually bumping into me. It takes a while to get out. It's really dark outside. The streetlights are barely working. The door locks behind me; exit only. I see a red bicycle leaning against the outside of the building. It's not attached to anything. Not locked up. I need to get home and I decide to take it. I hop on and then I notice it's a motorcycle. A big one. Bullet shaped. A Japanese model with everything up front and very little in the back. I start it up and start to ride away. It's incredibly easy to do. I don't know how to ride a motorcycle. Never have ridden one. I think I'm dreaming. I turn down an alley too sharply and run into the wall. It doesn't hurt and I start riding up the side of the wall. The bullet bike is fast and I can't control it. It flips off the wall and I'm falling but still riding the bike. It lands upright somehow and I'm still on top of it. I ride it out of the alley. On the sidewalk I look down and the bike is getting smaller and smaller turning into a miniature version of itself. I get off the bike and I m standing across the street from the Village. I didn't really go much of anywhere. Someone's yelling. They're yelling at me and running after me. It's the owner of the motorcycle. He's mad and he's coming after me. I'm afraid and I start to run away. I'm not getting anywhere, my legs will hardly move.

 I think I'm dreaming. That would explain it. I turn around and I'm angry now. Angry at myself for being afraid of a stupid dream. The motorcycle owner comes running up to me. He's yelling in my face and screaming about his motorcycle. I laugh at him. "You should relax." I say to him. "What you don't realize is that you are just a figment of my imagination." He stops. His face is twisted into a grimace but he's not screaming anymore. His head is shaved and he's wearing a red t-shirt. He looks tough but he's not moving. I'm not afraid of him anymore. "I'm dreaming and when I wake up, you won't exist anymore." I say to him.

"That's not true!" he yells back at me. "Gaaghhcnnnnnnuuhh!" his words are all garbled, he's not making sense anymore, but I can tell he is still trying to convince me that he's real. I turn around and walk away. The dream ends.

-

The knocking on the door had been so light he wouldn't have heard it all if he hadn't already been listening intently for the sounds of Shawn rumbling around in the kitchen. If the TV had been on or the shower had been going he wouldn't have heard the light tap tapping at all. It was morning and Ben was still in bed, preferring the relative warmth of the blankets to chill apartment air. Winter had come storming in officially with a snow that still clutched to the curbs and meager lawns of the Fan district in pathetic gray and white heaps; some of them waist high. The old apartment building's radiators were working at full tilt and they still barely managed to heat anything other than the five feet immediately surrounding themselves. Ben was still naked, having spent another night with Shawn. Shawn, Ben assumed, was busy brewing coffee in the kitchen. At least that was what the rumbling sounds and clinking glass had led Ben to believe.

The coffee was in preparation for their trip later on that morning. They had their day planned. First, a walk to the donation center, then off to the grocery store to cash their checks minus the obligatory 10 percent which they would undoubtedly spend on beer and ten cent packages of ramen noodles. Ramen noodles and peanut butter formed the bulk of Ben and Shawn's diet these past few weeks. Then maybe a trip to the Village for a plate of french fries and coffee or the rundown diner on third street if they were feeling like a change of scenery and a walk. The waitresses there were hotter than in the Village and often worth the walk. After that they would more than likely return home to watch one of Ben's VHS movies again and drink until they both passed out or Shawn made a pass at Ben; each option being equally likely.

Ben had been distractedly listening when he heard the knocking. Who would that be? He rolled over and inhaled deeply and sharply as he stretched within the confines of the bedclothes trying not to expose any unnecessary body parts to the wintry air. He listened, quietly waiting for Shawn to answer the door.

Ben heard the door creak open followed by muted voices one of them clearly Shawn and one of them vaguely female. There was a tentative familiarity in the exchange between them. Shawn's accent trilled up and down in an undefined expressiveness leaving Ben unable to discern what

Shawn and the disembodied female murmurs were talking about. Ben decided to brave the air outside and swung his naked legs out and over the side of the bed. He inhaled just slightly harder and deeper as his feet touched the cold wooden floorboards. He reached down and found his cold jeans to pull them up and onto his legs. He stood and pulled them up all the way deftly flipping his dick out of the path of his zipper's interlocking teeth as he pulled it closed without the marginal comfort his underwear would have afforded him. It was time to do his laundry again. He fastened his belt and scanned the room for his shirt as his nipples hardened despite the hair on his chest. He opted to go without it and wandered into the living room towards the kitchen in search of coffee and answers to the mysteries surrounding the vaguely female voice at the door.

When he got into the living Ben found Shawn and New Girl Judy sitting on the couch together chatting each other up as if the past three months of separation had never happened. They both talked easily and smiled as if New Girl Judy hadn't just disappeared and stopped calling with no explanation and even less regard.

"Hey Benny!" New Girl Judy said bubbling with a false enthusiasm that begged him not to acknowledge her previous absence.

"Hello." Ben replied without malice but not matching her enthusiasm. He briefly considered saying 'long time no see' but then decided that the cliché wasn't going to serve either of them very well. "Did you make some coffee?" Ben questioned Shawn instead.

"Kitchen." Shawn replied not taking his eyes off New Girl Judy.

"I know where it is." Ben said with an exaggerated voice trying to joke with an audience that was not paying any attention to him. They resumed their self-interested chatter as Ben waddled into the kitchen for his morning wake-up. His jeans sagged even with the belt on, down to a low that covered most, but not all, of his ass crack.

"Hey Benny," New Girl Judy called in from the living room. Ben wondered why she was all of a sudden calling him Benny as if that was a nickname he had always had. She was trying to get close to him. Or at least, affect a closeness between that had never existed. More than likely it was all wrapped up in her coming back. This was some part of her easing her way back from wherever the hell it was she had been. It was the sort of tactic that worked well with Shawn who made and lost friends easily. New Girl Judy wanted Ben to like her so she pretended to like him. Giving him a special nickname was her way of endearing herself to Ben. On another level it was a way of dominating him. Renaming him gave her some degree of power or position above him. "do you want to go to breakfast?" New Girl Judy finished.

"Where you goin'? Ben called back from the kitchen, shirtless and starting to shiver despite the sips from the scalding hot coffee in his hands.

"Somewhere far." Shawn answered back. "New Girl Judy's gonna give us a ride in her new car."

-

Ben ignored the indistinguishable world as it zipped past the window from the back seat of New Girl Judy's new car. The world slowly transitioned from a murky gray and white to a murky white with patches of occasional green and brown. Apparently they were going on a pleasure drive. Shawn and New Girl Judy sat up front and spoke back and forth. They volleyed clever observations and pseudo-witty remarks. They spoke at each other; each the star of their own particular show, reflected in the other's eyes. Ben found it difficult to get a word in and had, early on, resigned himself to awaiting their arrival at 'breakfast', whenever it came, quietly and without protest. Better to be ignored and silent than ignored and desperately grasping for attention.

Ben shifted uncomfortably on the warm tan leather interior of New Girl Judy's car. He felt unspeakably dirty in the newness of it. Dirty and ridiculously powerless. His ass was sweating something fierce and the state of the art seat warmers underneath him were set too high, even for the cold just outside. Ben was vaguely afraid his ass might start to stink or, even worse, leave a faint odor behind embedded in the leather. A permanent reminder of his disgusting presence. He wished he had showered this morning. He squirmed and repositioned himself again hoping to avoid a sweat stain on the leather. At least he was getting out of the city, he thought, and out of the house; wherever they were going.

-

"Well, I suppose you know." Shawn said with an air of apology that undercut itself with a snotty air. He slumped down into the couch next to Ben, leaving his quasi-apology hanging tin the air above them both.

"I knew the moment she got here. And even if I hadn't figured it out then, how could I not know now? That girl is loud." Ben's head was inclined towards the window. He still hadn't met Shawn's eyes with his own. New Girl Judy had let herself out this morning, promising to return in a few days. "Where was she anyway?" Ben inquired about her long absence, assuming that at some point during their romps last night she had told Shawn where she had been.

"She just went home. Didn't want to be here anymore." Shawn said referring to the city outside. New Girl Judy hadn't offered much more explanation to Shawn than she had offered to Ben the day before. They both supposed they needed to just accept what she gave. Shawn did.

"Listen, you're not upset are you?" Shawn asked finally broaching the subject that was hovering there.

"No." Ben lied. He was lying to Shawn but to himself as well. There wasn't any reason to be upset. He wasn't jealous. It wasn't jealousy that he was feeling. Was it? No, but it was close.

Something close to it. A distant cousin of jealousy. A relation of an unidentified want.

"You're not...jealous are you?" Shawn asked not wanting an answer. Not wanting to know the answer and afraid of the host of implications that answer would bring with it. He knew that if Ben was jealous that would mean they had been doing something more here, something Shawn was not ready for and would fight if he had to.

"No." Ben lied again with more conviction this time. "I just think I'm confused." I guess I thought...I don't know." Ben stammered through his words and tilted his head backwards to look at the ceiling. He was still avoiding eye contact. "We just never talked about girls I guess." He laughed lightly trying to mask the falsetto creeping into his voice. New Girl Judy's return had been a shock. An unexpected complication. Ben wasn't yet sure how he felt about it.

"What about girls?" Shawn asked.

"Like, do we sleep with girls?"

"Well, I do. You do what you want." Shawn said stiffly, this wasn't a conversation he ever thought he would be having with Ben. Ben was acting like a girl. "You do still want to sleep with girls don't you?" Shawn asked him.

"Well, yeah. But does this mean we're done with..." Ben trailed off again lacking the words to describe the exact nature of his relationship with Shawn these last two weeks. Ben looked over at Shawn.

"It doesn't have to be. Not if you don't want it to be." Shawn touched Ben's thigh with the back of his left hand. He started stroking it gently. It was an oddly tender gesture for Shawn and Ben felt mildly manipulated, but as he looked into Shawn's eyes he fell for it willingly.

"What do we tell people?" Ben asked.

"We don't have to tell them anything. We do what we want. That's all."

"So, do we keep it a secret?" Ben asked, he looked up at the ceiling again.

"Don't you think we should?" Shawn asked though it sounded more like a command than a question; an irrevocable truth that in his heart Ben knew already.

Ben was silent for a time and then replied. "Yeah. Yeah, I do."

14

It was wall to wall. Or rather, fence to fence. Or if you preferred; terminal limit of the communal backyard to the indistinguishable beginning of the dirty alley running in-between the streets. If anyone did bother to voice their opinion about what the precise limits of the party were their voice was drowned out by the slow dull din of clustered voices all vying for audibility in the backyard of a frozen winter's house party. It was too cold to stand outside for an hour or more but the crush of the crowd provided its own peculiar warmth. As the party progressed, the smoker's and keg runners had overwhelmed the otherwise small tight backyard and now there would be a hellish mess of cigarette butts and plastic cups to clean from the gray mud of the lawn tomorrow. Berto and lil Jim stood cloistered next to Fat Jenny and were determined to stay by her side. At least Berto was determined to stay by her side; lil Jim was determined to stay near Berto as he was the one person who would obligingly answer all of lil Jim's queries. Most everybody else just tried to ignore him.

Berto needed Fat Jenny though he wasn't fully conscious of it. Berto had circumnavigated the party twice with lil Jim in tow and failed to locate anyone he knew. They were both rather unsuccessful makers of small talk and parties always distilled into two essential elements: minglers and hubs. Minglers, like Berto and lil Jim, were either successful or not, they floated to and fro in the midst of the crowd like human flotsam soaking up interactions. Hubs, like Fat

Jenny, never moved. All things gravitated towards them and revolved around them. Parties, any party, indeed social gatherings of any kind, were impossible without them. Their networks of social contacts passed the word along and drew the crowd to any given destination of their choosing. How this all worked Berto had no idea, and was in fact completely unconscious of this quality to Fat Jenny's interactions. All Berto knew was that he needed to be near her. He had been sucked into her sphere of influence and now he orbited her as her network floated and mingled about her. All interactions mediated through and as a result of, his connection to her.

"I want a beer." Lil Jim said with words that condensed into clouds of vapor as they left his mouth.

"So go get one." Berto said not looking at him. Berto stared at Fat Jenny and Jack who were volleying jokes back and forth and until a few moments ago had been talking about rolling a joint. Neither of them were talking to Berto but he kept his attention poised on the two of them making him feel like part of the conversation anyway.

"Don't you want a beer?" Lil Jim asked Berto hopefully. He was in a daze and tottered woozily back and forth in the chill of the January night. It was a chill he didn't feel. He held a cigarette in his right hand that had stopped smoldering ten minutes ago, and an empty plastic cup that had once held a frothy, badly poured beer.

"No, I've still got mine." Berto replied still not looking at lil Jim. He consciously kept his voice flat and as emotionless as possible so lil Jim would have nothing to hold onto, conversationally speaking.

"Where do…." Lil Jim stammered, tottering still but determined to have a conversation with Berto even if Berto wasn't going to help. "Where do you think Shawn and Ben went?"

"Probably to go get beer." Berto said, hoping this would arouse lil Jim's interest and he would leave.

"I'm gonna go get beer." Lil Jim said as if he had been lost in ponderous reflection along this line fro some time; considering the pros and cons of his possible course of action. "You want to go get beer?" he asked after a pause.

"No man." Berto said impatiently, still attentively watching the conversation between Jack and Fat Jenny without participating.

"Okay." Lil Jim said as he clumsily shouldered his way into the surrounding crowd.

The keg was located just inside the house in a downstairs kitchen that opened onto the small deck where the original smokers had leaked outside from the party earlier in the evening. At least that was where lil Jim believed the beer to be. He couldn't quite remember and as drunk as he was, he could not be sure. He pressed on through the mass of bodies, jostled vigorously and bumped around by the bodies much bigger than his own.

"Hey." New Girl Judy said with a bigger than lil Jim smile as she turned around and recognized lil Jim. He had made it inside the house only to discover he been mistaken about the keg's location. He had moved through the kitchen and onward into a narrow hallway getting more or less stuck there by the now unmovable beast that was the party. New Girl Judy was there too.

"Do you know where Shawn is?" she asked, obviously as drunk, or drunker than lil Jim, slurring her speech as she cupped a translucent plastic cup with both hands. It was filled mostly with white foam floating over the light amber liquid lil Jim had come all this way to find.

"Do you know where the keg is?" lil Jim asked ignoring New Girl Judy's question as if he hadn't heard it at all.

"I think it's tapped." New Girl Judy said still smiling drunkenly. The pupils of her eyes opened wider in the dim light of the house party.

"Damn." Lil Jim said swaying slightly.

New Girl Judy lurched forward as someone bumped into her from behind. Her cupped drink sprayed white foam upward onto the side of lil Jim's face in the closeness of the hallway. She stepped even closer to him and placed a hand on his shoulder to steady herself. She dropped the hand left holding the beer lazily to her side and leaned in to speak into his ear placing most of her weight on his small frame. They were just about eye to eye height wise but she was slightly heavier than him due to her wider hips. "I got you all messy." She said and then licked the bitter froth off of the side of his face. New Girl Judy smiled into his shocked expression. "Cold." She said remarking on his skin temperature.

Lil Jim closed his eyes as she forced her tongue into his mouth and kissed him hard and sloppy. Too shocked for words, he said nothing as she led him out of the front door of the house; seemingly having no trouble at all navigating through the throng of people stuck there. There were a fair amount of people standing and slouching about the front stoop. They pushed through them effortlessly as well.

"Where are we going?" Lil Jim finally forced out through the sudden chill and the shock of the kiss. They were down the steps and cutting sideways across the lawn.

"No where." New Girl Judy replied leading lil Jim into an unoccupied and only mildly concealed spot amongst the chest high bushes along the front of the house. She turned and pushed him against the house. He complied clumsily.

Lil Jim puckered his lips unconsciously waiting for a kiss. His closed eyes shot open wide when he felt New Girl Judy's cold hands slide down the front of his pants.

"Cute little fucker." She said as she started to unzip his fly.

Lil Jim looked up at the people they had just pushed through on the porch that were still less than twenty feet away. They knew he and New Girl Judy were there. The fear and excitement bubbling in lil Jim's blood had sobered him up. He stared at the people smoking and talking through the leaves and branches of the evergreens he was in. They were speaking to each other and constantly stealing sideways glances at lil Jim's location with New Girl Judy in the bushes. Lil Jim knew the bushes concealed them somewhat but the porch people obviously knew they were there and probably saw enough to know what was going on when New Girl Judy kneeled down in front of lil Jim.

He was embarrassed and nervous and excited. His heart raced and a rush of fresh fear flooded through him, weakening his legs as he thought of everything the people on the porch could see. Then all the fear and excitement disappeared into a shining singularity of pleasure as his dick slid between New Girl Judy's lips. Lil Jim arched his head back and moaned softly and drunkenly as New Girl Judy gave him the first blow job of his life. Unasked for, and overly appreciated.

-

Shawn pulled out of Ben and rolled onto his back on the unfamiliar bed. They had snuck away, at Shawn's insistence, and locked themselves in this stranger's bedroom just a little while ago. It had seemed exciting at first, but now the imminent possibility that they might get caught was weighing in on Shawn. They were alone for now. But how long would it be before someone came up here looking for a bathroom or a discarded coat? Shawn wasn't even sure if he knew whose party this was. That might make it easier if they did get caught though. He didn't exactly want this getting around. This. What was this?

Shawn wasn't sure if he cared, as such, he just felt that people would judge him. And he didn't want that. The judgment. Maybe it wasn't the judgment so much. Maybe he just didn't want them knowing. But who were they? What would they know? Why did he care? He hadn't cared before. But no one really knew anything before. They knew something. But nothing, real. If anyone found out about this they would know something real for sure. He couldn't have that. "We should go." Shawn nudged Ben's cold sweaty back and rose up on the strange bed. He heard a light snore. "Get the fuck up!" Shawn whispered as loud as he could despite the fact that he had been moaning rather loudly a minute before.

Shawn stood up and started hastily dressing himself; an action facilitated by the fact that he had never gotten fully undressed in the first place. Ben rolled over, not fully naked himself but definitely woozy from drinking more than Shawn.

"We have to go." Shawn whispered again, loudly but with what approximated the effect of a quiet voice. He gave all the impression of a need for secrecy despite his utter inability to deliver that reality himself.

"Okay, okay." Ben said smiling his usual grimace. "Keep your pants on."

"No, you get yours on." Shawn replied not understanding that Ben was trying to make light of the situation their clandestine coitus had now put them both in. Shawn went to the door and listened intently to the incessant murmur coming form down the stairs. If they were lucky n one would be in the hall when they came out. The party hadn't yet gravitated upstairs. People were reluctant to invade the private space of the house's legitimate residents; unlike Shawn.

"I'm going." Shawn said. "You come out in a few minutes, okay?" Shawn said to Ben still in his exaggerated yet serious whisper.

"Okay." Ben said back in a mock whisper as if he were in a poorly staged sitcom.

Shawn opened the door and stepped out in to the hallway closing it behind him and not paying any attention to Ben. Ben sat alone in the dark waiting for at least a few minutes before following Shawn out.

15

"You're fucking Ben!" Fat Jenny told Shawn excitedly as if he himself hadn't known and had only been awaiting Fat Jenny's dramatic insight to reveal this unsightly truth. It had taken her awhile to put two and two together finally arriving at five. Her intuitive leap had finally lurched forward when Ben and Shawn returned to her private circle at the party a week ago. Only she had noticed the undone button on the fly of Ben's faded black jeans and had it been anyone else she would have dismissed it. People were always hooking up at parties and coming back from their hidden liaisons looking disheveled.

But not Ben. He never hooked up with anyone. The only loser she knew less likely to score at a party was lil Jim. And that, she knew, would never happen. Of course Ben could have been peeing and just be so drunk he couldn't button his pants properly. But he had come from the house, and Ben would never wade through a throng of blurry bodies to pee in a house he wasn't familiar with. He'd pee in the alley like any self respecting gutter dweller. Ben, she knew from personal experience, would just wander away quietly stumbling over the patchy brickwork in the alley between the row homes and the street, trying to avoid potholes when he could, but mostly not.

She had watched the two of them after that. Not obvious. They were quiet about it she noticed, but Ben couldn't hide it. And she could tell he was getting jealous of New Girl Judy.

"No, I'm not." Shawn said pointedly, keeping his voice flat and level as he looked Fat Jenny straight in the eye and waved smoke away with his left hand in Fat Jenny's living room. The purple couch underneath his ass creaked a little underappreciated whine in the silence between them.

"You sure are." Fat Jenny said and smiled delightedly breaking the silence. She knew she had him and read Shawn's expression easier than a comic book. The truth was right there and his firm voice and stare was just a cover up to try and convince her otherwise. He was trying to hard to keep his eyes fixed and his voice calm. This was all the proof she needed. She knew it all now. Knew everything as the whole story unfolded in front of her and formed like a storm cloud above her head. Of course, she thought to herself, after her visit. That's when it had all started. It had been a long and lonely break for them after all.

"Goody gum drops." Fat Jenny said. "This is great. Does New Girl Judy know? Are you and Ben dating now?" Fat Jenny stammered questions at Shawn without reserve, asking each one with a slight pause in-between that never lasted long enough for Shawn to begin to answer her.

"I'm leaving." Shawn said interrupting Fat Jenny's smiling questions, knowing that any further protest was useless. She knew. There was nothing he could do about it.

He couldn't make out why she was so happy. Was she happy to see him and Ben dating? Was she happy because she had figured it out and no one else had? Or was she just happy about getting to watch what this tender tidbit of gossip ready information was about to cause? A kind of self indulgent pleasure in watching the oncoming emotional fallout.

"Don't tell New Girl Judy." Shawn said. "I mean it." Shawn looked at Fat Jenny knowing she would tell New Girl Judy anyway, knowing he could do nothing to stop her.

-

Outline of a Dream:

It's a sunny day. Ridiculously beautiful out. I'm standing in a little field of grass. There's a tree

line behind me and the field itself is at a slight pitch that slopes downward towards the trees. It

also slopes gently upwards and ends at a road. It's a small two lane and there's another field

more densely populated by trees on the other side. Everything is green and blue in the world.

I have friends here. Their faces are blurry, but they all smile. I smile back, just happy to be here

I guess. I hear a low rumble. I look back across the road and off into the distance. There are

funnel clouds there. Huge and coming down to touch the ground. The clouds are swirling. They

spiral together. The rumble is becoming a roar and it keeps getting louder. I yell to my friends

that the tornado is coming. That we can't run. We won't get away. They all run and scatter

anyway. They can't hear me. The wind takes my voice. I look back at the oncoming whirlwind.

It's going to tear me to pieces. I can't imagine what that might be like. I doubt I will feel

anything. The whirlwind is so beautiful. The dream ends.

-

"So you will help me? You will help to get out?" Shawn asked again tentatively and honestly

humble without the tell tale traces of his "acquired" accent. The blissfully reassuring voice of

momanddad on the phone reiterated the terms of the deal he had struck and the money to follow.

It wasn't much, but it was a start, and it would facilitate his exit. His descent into decadence was

over. Finally.

He had lived out so many whims, he smiled now to think about them; but thinking about the

poverty he shuddered inside. It had been so hard, these past few months with Ben. Things had

almost gone beyond his control. But he was going to move away from all that at last. Away, and above it all.

-

"What do you mean you're leaving?" Ben asked incredulously disbelieving everything he had just heard. How could Shawn be leaving him now? Shawn had mentioned the house in passing a few times. Nothing serious; just idle conversations. His parents owned it. It wasn't much to look at. It had been owned by a dead relative and they had inherited it. Nobody had lived there in years but they had a neighbor keep it up for a modest fee. Shawn had explained the whole arrangement: his parent would put him back on the family payroll if he would leave town and live outside and away from 'bad influences'; presumably Ben. Ben was not invited, not by a long shot.

"I just can't keep doing this." Shawn said in reply as if this should answer all questions as to why he was leaving and planning not to come back.

"You're just afraid." Ben said, knowing on the one hand how true this was and on the other how incapable Shawn would be of admitting it.

"No I'm not." Shawn said as if he had read the words in Ben's head as Ben thought them. "I just can't keep living like this. I need to straighten out and get my life back together." Shawn looked around the dingy apartment they had lived in for months; fucking, eating, dragging on in boredom and sex, living together, doing whatever the hell it was they had been doing. He felt under-whelmed by it. It had all gone all too long.

"What's wrong with the life you have?" Ben said knowing he didn't want this answered. Shawn's life now was what Ben's had always been.

"I'm spinning out of control, I think." Shawn said after a short silence in which he suppressed the urge to say what he really felt.

"No you're not. Nothing has changed." Ben smiled a half-hearted grimace and looked at Shawn.

"Everything's changed. It's all gone crazy."

"But why?"

"Look, I just need to get out; that's all." Shawn had said this before, when he explained to Ben the deal he had made for his new financial fiefdom.

"Why can't I come too?" Ben asked. His voice shook lightly and he looked at the floor, rather than point his eye at Shawn.

"I just don't think that would be good for either of us. Things are getting weird."

"No. You mean it just wouldn't be good for you. You're getting scared. You're afraid of admitting what you are. What we are." Shawn and Ben both knew what had been going on, but neither of them had made any mention of it until now.

"Why are you acting like this? It's like you're a fucking girl or something."

"What the hell is that supposed to mean?" Ben said angrily.

"What I mean is. It's not like we were going out or anything." Shawn's snide English accent suddenly infuriated Ben.

"What the fuck were we doing then?"

"We were just fooling around is all."

"Fooling around. You call living with me, fucking me, taking all my money and eating my food just fooling around?" His comment about the food had been unwarranted and he felt instantly bad about it but Ben knew he couldn't take it back. He was losing Shawn and there was nothing he could do. The worst of it was that Ben knew he wasn't just losing Shawn he now stood to lose everybody. Shawn was Ben's hub; the center of his social network, and Shawn would take everyone, not just himself, away when he left the city.

"What?"

"What the fuck do I mean to you? Why the fuck did you move in here?" Ben yelled at Shawn still not looking at him.

"I needed a place to stay man. Back off." Shawn was getting nervous, afraid that Ben might get violent with him.

"What do you think we were doing?" Ben asked almost crying through his anger and making Shawn even more discomforted with this outward show of emotion.

"Like I said, just fooling around."

"Everything I did for you. To help you. I cared for you. How can you leave me now? After all this?" His voice pleaded with Shawn uselessly.

"I have to. I can't live like this anymore. I just can't do it. I just can't be this person." Shawn consciously tried to make his voice as sincere sounding as possible. He didn't mention the filth in the apartment, the poverty. It wasn't the person Shawn was afraid of; it was the money. He just couldn't stand the hopelessness that surrounded him here. Cheap noodles and beer everyday was fun for awhile but now it was over and he wanted out. And he was going to get out.

"You mean me. You just can't be like me." Ben said.

"I just can't do it any more. I can't live like this." Shawn repeated himself hoping he wouldn't need to elaborate.

"What do you mean?"

"I just mean I'm not like you."

"No…" Ben said. "You just have a way out. That's all."

-

New Girl Judy slumped heavily onto Fat Jenny's bed breathing loud and drunk beyond all repair.

Lil Jim and Berto rolled her over onto her back in the dim light coming in noiselessly from the living room of Fat Jenny's apartment. The four of them had been drinking all day but none of them as hard or as intently as New Girl Judy. She was on a mission. She had been ever since Fat Jenny had told her about Ben and Shawn and that had been a good two weeks now.

New Girl Judy had cussed Shawn out at first. Then walked away only to go back to Ben and Shawn's place and cuss them both out again. The second time full of cheap beer and smelling like Fat Jenny's weed. Ben, or course, stood there and took it without saying a word. Shawn had cussed back a little then just slammed the door in her face while she yelled in the hall outside the apartment. And that was the last she'd seen of him.

Lil Jim watched New Girl Judy's breasts rise and fall with each breath as she lay passed out on Fat Jenny's bed. It occurred to him that he hadn't thought to fondle them as she'd gone down on him at that party all those weeks ago. Not a word had passed between them about it despite the fact that he had been trying to get himself alone with her ever since then. Lil Jim figured he had a chance at her now that Shawn was out of the picture, and apparently into guys.

"She's so beautiful." Lil Jim said to Berto, knowing that Fat Jenny wouldn't hear from the living room where she was busy packing another bowl. She had told Berto and lil Jim to bring New Girl Judy in here; New Girl Judy had crashed here a lot in the past two weeks; ever since her confrontation with Shawn.

"Hmm." Berto hummed more than responded. He had little to say on the subject of New Girl Judy, figuring it wasn't possible to hook up with her as long as he was so involved with Fat Jenny.

"She's like an angel." Lil Jim said.

Berto thought this observation a little naïve. If New Girl Judy was an angel then Fat Jenny was fuckin' Buddha. Fuckin' Buddha, that's funny, Berto thought to himself and snickered.

Lil Jim's voice was barely above a whisper but it carried in the quiet light of the room. "You know, we hooked up at that party a couple of weeks ago."

"Really?" Berto's voice was raised a little with disbelief.

"I think I'm in love with her." Lil Jim said and the honesty of his voice made Berto want to laugh. What a stupid thing to say, he thought to himself. Then he heard the giggle. Berto looked and saw New Girl Judy shivering with an internal chuckle that she was no longer able to hold in. She had heard everything. She started laughing.

"Fucking little prick." New Girl Judy said as she stretched and laughed to herself a little more; then rolled over to go to sleep.

16

Ben and Shawn just stopped. Shawn moved out and stayed with Berto until they could make the move out of town. Lil Jim was already out at the house they were going to rent no doubt attempting to lay claim to one of the better rooms. The fact that Berto and lil Jim had been offered rooms to rent irked Ben but he was in no position to protest. No one would have listened anyway. Shawn would kick lil Jim out of whatever room lil Jim was wont to take; if Shawn decided he wanted it. After all it was his house. Berto drove the thirty two minute drive back and forth every two days and reported it to not be as far as Fat Jenny had claimed. Shawn tied up whatever loose ends he still had left in the city and talked with his parents fairly frequently leaving them both quite happy that he had decided to finally 'get his act together' in their words. When the money started flowing again, he was ready for Berto to move him out. Berto's lease would be up soon enough and then he would join lil Jim and Shawn out in the boonies. What they would do out there was anyone's guess but everyone agreed that Shawn's days of fucking up and doing drugs were in the past. He was finally growing up and getting his shit together.

-

Shawn, having left a few weeks earlier was not available to help Berto move and wouldn't have offered anyway. Ben showed up to help along with Fat Jenny and had secretly hoped he would get to see Shawn another time, but he was nowhere to be found. Ben had run into Jack and

Denny a couple of days previous and they had both called him a fag to his face. He didn't expect to see them here. It was quick move; most of the furniture had gone before. Fat Jenny had the last bags and was loading the mismatched mess into Berto's car. She was going to ride out with him and see the place tonight. She would probably crash there.

"Good luck out in the boonies man." Ben said amiably. He had no reason to dislike Berto, despite how much he envied him right now.

"Thanks, you too." Berto said distractedly. Unaware of the inconsistency in his response.

"I've always wanted to live in the country." Ben said looking up at the still slightly cool sky. It was early in the day and the sky was blue with few clouds. Spring was close but it was still idly chilly every few days.

"Why?" Berto asked, barely listening and rummaging in his trunk. "You have everything here. All within walking distance."

"I don't know. I guess it's just that I want to go somewhere, live somewhere I can smell grass and not hear some machine buzzing all the time in the background." Ben felt the words pour out of him. He didn't know why he was telling Berto this. Maybe telling Fat Jenny would be too burdensome. Maybe he knew she would just tell Shawn and they would both laugh. Maybe he just needed to tell someone, and he felt sure anything he said to Berto wouldn't go anywhere. Berto wouldn't tell anyone. Berto was barely listening. "I just want to choose where I go and not feel stuck all the time. Askin' for rides and always getting stuck in the backseat because no one really likes me. I just don't want to feel like I'm living in the fucking backseat anymore."

Ben said this and suddenly Berto realized what was really going on. He was watching the end of something that he had never even known existed. Ben and Shawn and everything that they were; Berto had never, really seen it. No one had; only Fat Jenny had found out the truth.

As they watched the last of Berto's possessions and badly packed bags getting tossed in the back of Berto's car, Ben looked up at Berto again through his hair with his one good eye squinting in the sun. "I just can't believe Shawn left me." Ben smiled idly and walked away having already said his goodbyes to Fat Jenny who sat roughly in the front seat causing the car to bounce ever so slightly.

"Hey... later days man. ", Berto called out with the familiar parting words everyone in the clique had been using of late. He waved a goodbye, unsure of when he would next see Ben.

Ben spun around halfway on his left heel. His stringy brown hair covered the side of his face. He had shoved his hands deep into the pockets of the jeans he had been wearing for a few days. Berto could see his hands balled into fists. He lifted his shoulders in an almost imperceptible shrug without taking his hands out of his pockets and his brown stained t-shirt lifted and rose revealing just a hint of his hairy belly underneath. A slightly chill wind blew through the alley making ripples in a puddle of water at Ben's feet. His t-shirt was too thin for the weather. "Days later man...days later." he said and turned back around to shuffle down the alley, shivering towards home.

"Days later." Berto mumbled to himself giggling a little at the play on words. He watched Ben walk away, not knowing where he was going. Not really caring at all.

www.ingramcontent.com/pod-product-compliance
Lightning Source LLC
Chambersburg PA
CBHW052145170626
46812CB00004B/1599